The Earth, Mungongoh And The Dwarf Revolt

Colin Diyen

Langaa Research & Publishing CIG
Mankon, Bamenda

Publisher:
Langaa RPCIG
Langaa Research & Publishing Common Initiative Group
P.O. Box 902 Mankon
Bamenda
North West Region
Cameroon
Langaagrp@gmail.com
www.langaa-rpcig.net

Distributed in and outside N. America by African Books Collective
orders@africanbookscollective.com
www.africanbookcollective.com

ISBN: 9956-728-79-9

DISCLAIMER
All views expressed in this publication are those of the author and do
not necessarily reflect the views of Langaa RPCIG.

Dedication

*This book is dedicated to Aloysius Akoni Diyen,
Sister Mary Gladys Diyen, Cyprian Nkessa Diyen
and Benjamin Diyen*

*I won't forget my Bambinios and able assistant
editors; Ndam Ghozt Betrand; Diyen Kini Maya; my
noble daughter, Ndam Nange Marie Cecile; and my
little sparrow, the very great Diyen Momjang Ayeah.*

Prologue

Awobua, the king of a small rocky satellite of Mars, known as Mungongoh, had a life's goal, and this was to rid Earth of all humans and transfer his subjects to it. All the top brains in Mungongoh had been concentrated in an institution meant for the development of ideas to conquer Earth, popularly known as the IRDI or Institute of Research for the Development of Ideas. This institution had come up with various diabolic ideas, hideous enough to make Lucifer jealous that he was not the author; but, apart from causing much sorrow on earth, they had never actually proved efficient enough to rid the Earth of all mankind. They had introduced the Spanish, Bird, and Swine flus. They had devised plagues, Ebola, HIV/AIDS, and many others. They had even introduced a weapon of mass destruction, the neutron bomb, which would have completely cleared Earth of humans if their plans had come out as intended.

Mungongoh maintained permanent watch over Earth to determine ways to destroy it. It organized spying expeditions to Earth on a regular basis. For their journeys to Earth, they used flying saucers that were so swift they were not discernible by the human eye. Each member of the IRDI had access to these space vehicles, and could send agents to the earth for information gathering or destructive purposes.

The shortcomings in these ideas had resulted in failure, and this had raised the fears of the members of the IRDI to the highest limits as they were fully aware of how much the king was burning for success. Fortunately for them, the king regularly took out his frustrations on his servant dwarfs, who were generally the ones in the way when his fists went flying. Apart from being used as side stools, the dwarfs provided whatever service the king wanted. They were the only persons allowed to serve the king's favourite drink, *mukal,* whenever he ordered it.

Mobuh, King Awobua's flabby chief minister, was his main liaison with the people of Mungongoh and paid total allegiance to him. As in most countries and big organizations, Mobuh had a few protégées that he had pushed into high positions. A clear example was Professor Itoff, the head of the IRDI, whose life Mobuh had succeeded in persuading the king to spare after several failures by the IRDI to produce results. Other prominent members of the IRDI were Dr. Funkuin, Fulumfuchong, Yivissi, and Dr. Kini.

There were two notable non-members of the IRDI. Ngess was a simple man who had the ability to assess correctly and deduce the right outcome, but - like Cassandra in ancient Troy - his opinion was always sought only after a seemingly impeccable idea had failed. Nyamfuka was a handsome spy employed by Dr. Funkuin.

King Awobua kept ferocious lions as pets, and the mangled bodies of dwarfs that he hammered to death in his vicious outbursts of anger were provided as choice titbits to them. Mungongoh citizens suspected of treason ended up there too. A few of the members of the IRDI who were blamed for having failed to provide the king with the opportunity to take over the earth also met with death through the champing jaws of the lions.

The last great idea developed by the IRDI was a massive offensive against Earth, involving the use of every pestilence available and the neutron bomb. To achieve this, agents were dispatched in great numbers to Earth to smuggle out to Mungongoh every material that could be used in this massive offensive. When some of these agents were apprehended and the disappearance of nuclear materials, samples of deadly viruses, and other dangerous items was discovered, there was general panic.

A crises meeting of the super powers was summoned by the President of America, where it was decided that there should be a general alert and complete unity among nations. This meeting had been closely monitored by King Awobua, who discovered that, although the earthlings were still fogged as to the origin of their problems, they were determined to fight back. Prodded by a suggestion from Dr. Kini, one of his academics, the king decided to order the suspension of the offensive against Earth. All Mungongoh agents were withdrawn and all flying saucer expeditions to Earth ceased. King Awobua was waiting for the earthlings to become complacent and forget about the threat from outer space before striking.

On Earth, nations improved their collaboration with each other and ceased all aggressive acts. North and South Korea operated on the most cordial terms. China buried the war hatchet with Taiwan, and the Dalai Lama, who was now living in Tibet, visited China often. The Israelis were assisting Palestine through a lot of construction work and had embassies in all the Arab countries, while the Arabs were now speaking about Israel on the friendliest terms. Strategic factories for the production of weapons of mass destruction and other arms were transformed into giant factories for the production of house hold goods and other harmless but useful items. Even the Soviet Union had jettisoned communism and totalitarianism, and the various socialist republics that had existed within the union were now independent democratic countries.

The nations of the earth actually became complacent and completely forgot about the threat from outer space as Awobua had expected. After making a great effort and allowing more time than previewed to elapse, Awobua was provoked by the lavish live styles and ceremonies on Earth to resume his diabolic plans. The IRDI went back to work.

Fulumfuchong, one of the members of the IRDI, had had enough. He developed a clever scheme of enlisting the help of the earthlings to overthrow Awobua and put an end to the regime of terror. He carried out this move with the help of the Americans and ended up as king in place of Awobua. His next move was to reward his accomplices and establish a new reign in Mungongoh.

1

The first meeting under the new regime of the Institute of Research and Development of Ideas (IRDI) to take over Earth was held in the palace. The room was large enough, and a real throne had been set up at one end. The throne was composed of two huge, comfortable seats, carved out of some rich glittering material, upholstered with soft rich velvet 1 and stuffed with well-processed hair from lions' mane. Lion pelts had been well arranged as foot rugs, and side stools of marble were provided. The throne was on a raised platform, facing the rest of the room, which had been transformed from Awobua's lonely abode to a lively royal court and reception room. The importance of this first meeting of the IRDI warranted that it should take place here.

Fulumfuchong sat smiling in his royal robes while the queen, Yivissi, was resplendent by his side. The other members of the IDRI were all present, apart from Professor Itoff, whose important position was now taken by Dr. Funkuin. In his capacity as chief minister and key adviser to the king, Ngess was seated directly opposite Funkuin. The other members of the IRDI occupied seats on both sides of the marble table, all with small monitors in front of them. There were a few additions to this august assembly. Having been appointed into the newly created position of chief diplomat, Nyamfuka had automatically earned a place in the assembly. The other two were bright young fellows whose full confirmation as members of the elite team would come later, if their participation was rated as up to standard.

Dwarfs had been given seats in a corner where they sat attentively waiting, ready to serve the king or his guests at the slightest notice. The dwarfs were still virtually slaves, but there had been some improvement in the way they were treated.

This meeting was considered very important for several reasons. It was to be the last meeting of the IDRI as the lust for Earth was no longer top priority on the list of the desires of the new king. Actually, taking over Earth from the humans was far from the ambitions of Fulumfuchong, who rather preferred close collaboration with Earth.

The king cleared his throat, an indication that he wanted the meeting to start.

"You are all very welcome here," Fulumfuchong declared. "You are all aware that we don't have coronations often because of our extended lifespan, and this makes them very lavish and ceremonious. In this particular case, we have just delivered Mungongoh from a tyrant and are planning a new regime. Since Mungongoh has already accepted me as king, I no longer consider a coronation ceremony important. We shall, therefore, skip that aspect and go ahead."

He turned to his new bride, the queen, and smiled, as if to get her support for the scrapping of the coronation ceremony.

She nodded in acquiescence. Most women would have cherished the idea of a lavish and grandiose affair that would make them a figure of admiration to all the members of their sex, making others outright jealous; but Yivissi was not fond of lavish ceremonies.

Encouraged by her reaction, the new king continued.

"This meeting is convened to make Mungongoh a better place. We shall all put our heads together and contribute fully to achieving this."

He paused to look round and make sure that everybody was attentive and taking in his points.

Satisfied, he continued. "You shall no longer have a lonesome recluse for king. The king shall be open, receptive, and officially married. You shall now have a queen. Yivissi here is the queen."

There was heavy applause from the assembly of tough eggs.

The king beamed broadly. The enthusiasm was really encouraging. Mungongoh had always had kings, but nobody ever knew with whom the king consorted to have an heir. There were no official princes, therefore, and the heir was only brought out when the king died. This crude system was developed to prevent mothers of prospective kings from transforming themselves into queens and claiming the throne at the death of the king. It was also a means of eliminating the possible official existence of princesses who could equally aspire to the throne if the king ended up producing only female children. Besides, in this manner, the king was not tied to one woman. He was made to secretly mate with several, who during that period had no access to other men. This guaranteed that royal blood was indeed transmitted into the future king, and that at least one male child would be produced. Since the male children were taken away immediately after they were born, no connection remained between mother and child, and so no presumptuous woman could boast that she was the mother of the king. These male babies, taken and secretly groomed, ensured that at least one of them would be ready when the need for a king arose.

"I shall proceed by officially installing our biggest officials of Mungongoh into their functions." He beckoned at Ngess, who limped up to the king and knelt in front of him.

"Ngess," said the king authoritatively, "You are from this day installed as chief minister of the regime and key adviser to the king."

"Thank you, sir," replied Ngess, standing up and going back to his seat.

"Professor Funkuin," the king said, smiling at the new head of the IRDI.

"Yes, sir," Funkuin answered, moving up to kneel in front of the king.

"Remember, I called you professor. You now have the highest academic title in the land," the king said graciously.

"Thank you, sir," Funkuin replied solemnly.

"You are now officially the head of the IRDI or whatever institution we decide to transform it into." The king was still smiling. "And I wish to state here that we don't hate Earth any longer. There is no need for hate sciences. If I call you professor, I am considering the fact that you have a solid base in history and knowledge of Earth. To hate Earth, you had to have thorough knowledge about it. Now you will use that knowledge to work with it. You are now Professor of History."

"I am grateful, sir," she replied, returning to her seat.

The king turned to Nyamfuka, "Nyamfuka, please, step up."

Nyamfuka moved up to the king and knelt in front of him.

"You are no longer a mere field agent that is sent to Earth on spying missions," the king said. "You are now a senior minister in charge of relations with Earth and a full member of the IRDI."

Nyamfuka was too overwhelmed to utter a word. He simply got up respectfully and went back to his seat.

"Any other appointments will be made known with time after I consult with my key advisers," the king said. "It shall take several meetings to come up with a new Mungongoh.

Ngess will give us a rundown of our various topics of discussion."

Ngess concentrated on the monitor in front of him. There was no keyboard, but his concentration seemed to type out something that appeared on all the monitors in front of the members of the IRDI. It was the list of various topics that had been developed for discussion. He proceeded to read out loud.

"The IRDI needs a new name, status, and function," Ngess read.

The new senior minister lifted up his head and looked around as surprise was registered on the faces of the members of the IRDI. The king signalled for him to continue.

"This will be followed by a discussion of what we want our relationship with Earth to be like," Ngess continued. "In short, we are tracing the path for Nyamfuka to follow. Then, we shall consider certain aspects which may not have meant anything to us up till now, such as sports, tourism, religion, arts and culture, and the identification of historical sites of Mungongoh. We are far more advanced than the earthlings in many things; but, in some simple aspects that we have carelessly overlooked, we simply have to learn from them."

"Does anybody think that we should add any other item?" the king asked

"I was thinking about our dwarfs," said Yivissi.

"Ah yes, the dwarfs," said Ngess. "That is quite important. We shall add it for discussion."

Ngess was through. He turned towards his king.

"For now, we shall adjourn and let our newly appointed officials get fully installed in their offices," the king said. "That way, each person will be capable of playing his or her rightful role during the next meeting. I intend to summon the next meeting in a week's time. It shall still be held here in the palace. And the following meetings shall be held here until we have laid a solid foundation for the new Mungongoh. I recommend that we do as much Earth watching as possible so that we return with valuable contributions concerning our future relationship with it."

The king turned and looked at Yivissi meaningfully.

The new queen stood up smiling. "We shall make our meetings lively and socialize better. No more lonely drinks of mukal in the palace. We shall be served drinks and snacks of everybody's choice at the end of meetings."

She turned to the dwarfs. "Get on with it, little fellows," she said

The dwarfs immediately became busy making sure that each person was served.

The following week was busy for everybody. While Ngess was adjusting to his role of chief minister and Funkuin was adjusting from hate sciences to the role of professor of history, Nyamfuka was updating his knowledge of Earth. He had been out there on many missions, but there was still much that he needed to learn.

2

Finally, the week was over and the members of the IRDI came together for the next meeting. The participants travelled to the palace in fast cars that seemed to float along noiselessly. They all filed into the palace and took their seats accordingly.

"Ngess, what are we discussing today?" the king asked when everybody had settled down

"We shall start with the new name for the IRDI, sir" Ngess replied

"Yes," declared the king. "It is very important to come up with a more conducive name. The IRDI was created by King Awobua to give him ideas on how to destroy the earth and transfer us there. In our blind thirst for a better place in which to live, we all supported him in this wild ambition. Now, we are rather planning to be on the friendliest terms with the earth and prefer peace to war. To achieve his aims, King Awobua chose the members of the IRDI carefully. The top brains of Mungongoh all became members of this institution, and you are all here present. Instead of dissolving the IRDI completely therefore, I would prefer the other option of keeping it under another name and function. What do you honourable ladies and gentlemen think? Let us have ideas. Should we simply close down the IRDI, maintain it, or transform it into something else?"

"Let's hear about the new name and function," said Funkuin hastily, hoping for something equally big that would not tamper with her very high position.

"The floor is open for debate," said the king.

"Awobua is no longer king, and the lust for the Earth is no longer a priority here," said one of the old bald professors about to retire from active service. "Since the primary reason for the creation of this institution was to conquer the Earth, it no longer has any reason to exist. We should, therefore, simply scrap it."

"Yes!" shouted another old chap who had been next in rank to Itoff and was terribly pained by the fact that Funkuin had superseded him. "The king is intelligent and level-headed enough to make key decisions, even if faced with complications. Apart from that, he has advisers."

"Mungongoh will face a lot of delicate decisions, especially now that we have to coexist with the Earth," said Nyamfuka. "Let us transform the IRDI into another institution as proposed, but this time, instead of ideas to conquer the earth, we shall bring up ideas that will guide us to coexist and collaborate positively with the Earth."

"I think the institution should stay, but under another name and with a different key function as proposed by the king," said Dr. Kini, one of the young members of the elite team. "I have all due respect for the king and accept that he has the capacity to make sound decisions, but no one man is clever enough."

At this point the king put his hand up and the debate ceased immediately. Everybody subsided into respectful silence. Fulumfuchong smiled. Power was good. You had respect, even from persons who might be far better than you.

"I have heard your arguments and I must admit that your opinions all carry some weight. However, we still have lots of other items on the agenda and need to move on." The king removed his cap, put it on the stool by his side, and continued. "King Awobua was not foolish when he created the IRDI. We all considered him the wisest person in Mungongoh, and he had Mobuh and others to advise him on how to conquer the Earth. Yet, he counted more on ideas developed by the IRDI to accomplish his ambition. You would agree with me, too, that many of the ideas developed by us were quite ingenious and would have worked if not for the fact that the earthlings are quite smart. One could even say that the God of the Christians, Moslems, Hindus, and Buddhists is protecting them."

King Fulumfuchong smiled at this last wise crack.

"Besides," he continued, "Mungongoh has been in a stagnant situation, completely devoid of change, for a very long time. Our technology, though considerably better than what exists on earth, was inherited from our ancestors, way back during the era of Mars. Since then, there has been little improvement. On the other hand, we simply live, eat, and work. We may not have realized that we have had quite a dull life all along because it has been our way of life. If you took a holiday on Earth, you would discover that we live dull lives, without bustle and excitement. Although there is much sorrow and misery on Earth, they know how to live, have fun, and enjoy themselves."

"The king is right," said Nyamfuka, trying to make it look as if he was not interrupting the king. "Some earthlings have even developed the principle of living fast and dying young. Where life could be drab, earthlings brighten it up with various forms of entertainment. Virtually everything is transformed into one form of entertainment or another. Some earthlings amuse themselves by taking hard drugs and feeling high. Others spend the day abusively drowning in alcohol despite the consequence of nursing a disturbing hangover and splitting headache the next day."

"Our new senior diplomat knows what he is talking about," said the king. "During my short stay down there with Yivissi, I noticed that many of those perverts on earth called voyeurs have lots of fun watching others - even animals -

having sex, whereas they could have simply gotten a partner and enjoyed it themselves."

"I am not sure those are normal persons," said one stern looking female. "They need their heads checked."

"You may think that," said Nyamfuka, "but many on earth call it fun. Sex watching constitutes quite a huge industry, and much money is invested in it."

Ngess took a sip from the glass in front of him, licked his lips, and looked at the king, an indication that he wanted to continue with the meeting.

"We were saying," the king concluded, "that the earthlings can enjoy anything as long as they transform it or make it look interesting. That is why they can spend so much time absurdly admiring waterfalls and ugly jagged landscapes and being excited over old useless pieces of art and antique items. They spend a lot of time and money on games that consist of hitting balls with their feet, arms, and clubs - just for fun or for competition. Actually, we need as many hands as possible on deck to transform Mungongoh into what the earthlings call heaven. Let's transform the IRDI into an institution to achieve this."

"But what shall we transform the IRDI into?" enquired one of the old, scrawny females.

"Another institution," replied Ngess, "but this time we shall have a very useful one. I propose that we call it the 'Academy of Ideas for the Development of Mungongoh' or AIDM."

"What of the 'Academy of Ideas for Collaborating with the Earth or AICE?" proposed Nyamfuka, the chief diplomat.

"Although the IRDI completely concentrated on the Earth," replied Ngess, "we are thinking of something bigger, something that takes into consideration relations with other planets that we may end up knowing, and not forgetting the improvement of Mungongoh itself. We don't want an institution that is limited in scope."

"So, collaboration with the Earth will just be part of its activities?" asked Yivissi

'Quite so," replied Ngess.

"Who has other ideas?" asked the king.

"I think Ngess is right," said Funkuin. "He simply needs to elaborate more on the roles of this institution."

"Is it going to be some kind of parliament, bundestag, Knesset, or congress as they have on Earth?" asked a female academic.

"Not really," replied Ngess. "I am looking at something more in line with an institution where much research is carried out, combined with much thinking, and resulting in conception and concrete ideas. A parliament only debates and argues, with each side condemning whatever is presented by their opponents, whether it is correct or not."

Everybody was looking at Ngess for more. None of them had ever guessed that such a lowly man could so efficiently occupy such a high position and perform so excellently.

"This will be some kind of elite group, not necessarily pretending to represent the people like the parliaments on Earth. You don't make laws, you don't vote budgets. You rather develop ideas that will directly improve the lives of the people of Mungongoh. That is why you are not like the bunch of halfwits or rich arrogant fellows that use power, money, and honeyed tongues to convince poor, ignorant fellows to vote them into parliament and keep them there. You are not elected but selected. You are selected on merit, on the basis of your output, not your capacity to throw money around or fight the other camp."

Everybody was awed by this display of intelligence. Mobuh would not have come anywhere near this.

"I think Ngess has said it all," the king said. "All we need to do now is set up a small committee headed by Ngess to set up detailed modalities on this new institution. We all agree that it will be called the Academy of Ideas for the Development of Mungongoh, abbreviated as AIDM, and the head of the AIDM remains Professor Funkuin."

A print out of this new royal decree was immediately made available for the royal seal. Drinks were passed round to celebrate the birth of a new institution.

"It looks like our meetings shall now be quite interesting," whispered a happy fellow sitting next to Nyamfuka.

"Certainly," Nyamfuka whispered back, beaming broadly. "And our new king is bent on making life quite easy and enjoyable for us. *La dolce vita,* as earthlings in Italy would say."

The meeting was adjourned for another week.

3

As decided by the king, the next meeting was still held in the palace.

"We have dissolved the IRDI and now have the AIDM," the king declared. "This meeting now continues as the first meeting of the AIDM."

The king turned to Ngess who was concentrating on the monitor in front of him. "Ngess will continue with the next topic."

Ngess cleared his throat, checked his monitor, and said, "The next item here concerns diplomacy. We are certain that none of the nations that lived alongside our forefathers in Mars survived the holocaust. We have not identified any other planet apart from Earth where there are living beings with which we can have any kind of relationship. Our discussions here will, therefore, be limited to our relationship with the earthlings for now. The floor is open."

"Maybe we should bring in some of our agents who have long experience as operatives on Earth," suggested a professor with a walrus moustache.

"That is not necessary," said Nyamfuka. "I was recently an agent on Earth and believe some of you sitting here have taken field trips to Earth to acquaint yourselves with certain facts. Besides, from my knowledge of the activities of the defunct IRDI, watching Earth was a compulsory part of your duties even though you mostly did it from your monitors here in Mungongoh."

"Nyamfuka is right," said king Fulumfuchong. "We know enough in this room about Earth."

"I would propose a cautious move in this line." said Funkuin. "Let's maintain our relationship only with the Americans for a while."

"For how long?" asked a thickset professor. "If we want to make friends with earthlings, then let's make friends with earthlings, no limitations."

"I back Professor Funkuin's idea of caution," said the professor with the walrus moustache. "We can't just open up our small country to everybody. Imagine for yourself how America and Europe raided the poor African countries when they had the chance."

"That was called colonialism and, later on, imperialism," the thickset professor offered. "Their imperialistic tendencies could be stretched to us, especially if we deal only with America. On the other hand, we can have fair treatment if we coerce several earthling nations into competing for our friendship."

"If we give the least room, we might be overrun by Chinese, Indians, Pakistanis, and Latinos," said king Fulumfuchong. "The migratory tendency of these peoples has been largely demonstrated on Earth. So long as there is hope for business or a better life in a possible host country, they will move on."

"Before we continue with our discussion," said Nyamfuka, "let us all understand what a diplomatic relationship is all about. It could mean that you open an embassy and keep representatives there. In response to this, the countries with which you have such a relationship would install embassies here with their diplomats, who would all enjoy a certain status. A diplomatic mission is comprised of several attachés in various fields, such as culture, trade, the military, etc. These diplomats come in with their families and dependents. We could be expecting quite a crowd. On the

14

other hand, having diplomatic missions abroad could be quite an expensive affair and would tell much on the budget of the country."

"I suggest we give this up," said a lady with a screechy voice. "All those diplomats will move in with all the decadence of Earth. Imagine what will happen to our little girls."

"And our little boys, too," said the man next to her.

"Little boys?" enquired another female. "You mean that while those lechers from Earth go for innocent girls their women go for boys?"

"The fear is not from the women," said her neighbour. "The male lechers have no limits. While some prefer girls of very youthful ages, others go for boys. Even our men are not spared as some prefer lovemaking with adult men."

"That is quite true," insisted the professor with the walrus moustache. "Imagine the type of scenes we watched during Yivissi's ... I am sorry ... the queen's presentation at the IRDI when she wanted to prove to us that the decadence on Earth had reached such an alarming extent that it would be easy to convince their God to crush them in anger. I tell you; even our wives would be exposed to horny diplomats."

"What do you take us women for?" shouted a female with reddened lips. "By your statement, you give the impression that we are all sluts and bitches."

"And we have no law courts to try them like they have on Earth," said Ngess hastily, in a bid to prevent more females from protesting. "Even if we had, they would all have some degree of diplomatic immunity."

"But our agents have operated over there for ages and have never been really corrupted," said Nyamfuka. "What makes you think that the presence of a few diplomats here will change anything? We might end up changing them into better men and women instead."

"Not those earthlings," said Funkuin. "They are always too wicked, too greedy and selfish, too sneaky, too horny, too pretentious, or too lazy and negligent. Very few of them have that uprightness that comes from the heart. Bringing them in to mingle with our people on an almost permanent basis will be quite risky."

"That is the real situation," the King said in support. "Besides, we have a different life span from the earthlings. May I remind all of you what happened when a few of the American soldiers who had assisted us in knocking off Awobua stayed here for a short while before leaving? Before we knew it, a few of our girls were pregnant. Now we don't know how the children will turn out when they are born or how long they will live."

"We could consider that an experiment," said Nyamfuka jokingly. "After all, some of our horny agents operating on earth might equally have gotten quite a number of earthling women pregnant, and we have never bothered to know the consequences."

There was some general laughter.

"That is a serious point we have always overlooked," said Ngess. "I suppose many of those dwarfs from perfectly normal parents on Earth are a consequence of the promiscuous attitudes of some misguided Mungongoh agents. The earthlings often dismiss such irregularities at birth as a result of mutations. If they knew better, there would be much worry."

"That," explained the king, "is the reason why we sent only male agents to earth. You see, there was always the fear that females might bring back a pregnancy from an earthling male, and we would be faced with the present predicament left behind by the American soldiers. On the other hand, we never bothered about what was happening out there on earth."

"I had always recommended that we have all our operatives on earth undergo a vasectomy," said one stern looking old chap. "Unfortunately, my opinion was never considered. Now that we intend to set up diplomatic missions on Earth, we should be prepared for more trouble."

"I, too, have something to say on that point," the queen said, surprising everybody.

Her new status as queen had made everybody forget that she had been a member of the IRDI and had not been relieved of the position before it was transformed into the AIDM.

"I totally object to allowing earthling residents here," she said, speaking with some authority now. "The earthlings have an abusive life style and always over indulge. Either they drink too much, use drugs too much, or are over-sexed. Let them loose here, and they shall start spawning earthlings with our young females. With their influence, we shall soon have beer bars with bawdy maids and even brothels. This will be followed by organised robberies. We are already overwhelmed by the petty thefts of food and clothing items we often suffer at the hands of the dwarfs. Earthlings also have a tendency to challenge constituted authority. They may easily end up sponsoring an uprising or an attempt on the king's life. We are certainly condemned to deal with them, but we must be very careful."

"The queen has said something quite important," Ngess said. "She is quite right about the way we should deal with the Earthlings. I, too, propose that we act with a lot of caution. We can set up embassies in a few key countries such as America, Russia, Great Britain, Germany, France, Nigeria,

South Africa, Saudi Arabia, Japan, India, China, Australia, and Brazil. On the other hand, we shall permit diplomats from these countries to come in only on brief visits during which their movements shall be closely monitored."

"Are you sure the earthlings will agree to that?" Funkuin asked.

"They will have no choice," Nyamfuka replied. "Their lust for the various types of shinny pebbles strewn all over Mungongoh and the minerals that are abundant in our rocks will push them to accept anything, just to get their hands on these items."

"What of your choice of countries where we should set up embassies? What criteria did you use to make these choices?" Funkuin asked, looking directly at Ngess now.

"I think I can answer that," said Nyamfuka.

He turned to Ngess. "Sorry for the interruption, sir, but I just thought that I could explain better since I have been out there often, whereas you have never travelled beyond Mungongoh."

"No problem at all," said Ngess. "Go ahead."

"Thank you, sir," said Nyamfuka and continued. "Because of high costs, we cannot have embassies in every country on Earth. On the other hand, we need to touch all the continents. I have been to Earth on many missions, and I did not move with my eyes and ears closed. The countries mentioned here are the most prominent countries in each continent.

"The proposal therefore is that, apart from our ally America, we develop diplomatic relationships with the other countries mentioned by Ngess?" asked the king.

"Quite so," replied Nyamfuka, the senior diplomat of Mungongoh.

"And how do we go about it?" demanded one of the female professors. "You know, on Earth they have schools where they groom diplomats. They have certain procedures."

"I think Nyamfuka is capable of handling that," said Funkuin. "He has had much exposure and will know what to do. I propose we send him to Earth, accompanied by a few members of the AIDM, to meet the presidents of these countries and propose our collaboration with them. I won't mind being on this mission myself."

Her intimacy with Nyamfuka was no longer a secret although they were not yet husband and wife.

"Now that we are thinking of close collaboration with the Earth," said Nyamfuka, "Maybe we should start considering the earthling saying that 'He who wants peace must prepare for war.'"

"What do you mean?" asked Yivissi, rather frightened

"I was thinking of an army like they have in all countries on Earth."

"An army?" asked the king. "We are peaceful enough without an army. Bring in soldiers and trouble will come."

"What if the earthlings attack?" asked Ndaba.

"Youngblood!" said Ngess. "Always hot. We have our natural defences already. We are far off from Earth and will easily detect any spaceships coming in. Besides, the chaps on Earth all want peace now."

"Then why do they develop huge arsenals and recruit lavishly into their various armies?" asked Funkuin. "The human mind is always calculating and full of intrigues. We can't trust them an inch. However, I am opposed to a standing army. Let us consider reinforcing other options we have to protect ourselves."

"Give us a hint," said Ngess.

"On Earth, they have custom officials at all ports of entry into each country," said Nyamfuka. "These officials are not soldiers but have the role of checking for contraband or banned items and preventing them from being smuggled in. Any suspicious object brought in by any earthling diplomat shall be confiscated."

"We shall have special monitors at each port, which shall scan all ships approaching from the Earth to make sure that we have a thorough idea of what they are carrying so that we can counter every attempt on time," the king added.

"That means we don't need soldiers," said Nyamfuka. "But what of police?"

"We have enough order in Mungongoh," said Ngess. "Generally, on Earth the presence of a police force is often accompanied by lawlessness and disorder. Once you bring in the forces, people are compelled to start breaching the law to give them work and a reason for existing."

"We can transform the king's guards into some small force for the purpose of coping with possible atrocities from the earthlings," said Funkuin. "Some of their bad habits may rub off on a few citizens."

"That is quite correct," said the queen. "We need some kind of protection if those earthlings are to be allowed here in Mungongoh."

"Diplomats are supposed to be dignified persons," Nyamfuka said. "They are supposed to use fine language and sound very polite. I don't believe we shall have much trouble from them."

"We shall suspend that topic for now and come back to it later," said the king. "Our next meeting is in a week's time as usual. We shall start with sports."

The meetings were now quite exciting and every member was anxiously looking forward to them. As they came in and sat down for the next meeting, they all noticed that the king and queen were dressed in beautifully designed matching dallas.

"That attire is wonderful, sir," Ndaba said, followed by a general round of admiration from the other members.

Yivissi was quite radiant and wore earrings of emerald.

The king smiled gracefully, asked for the meeting to start, and reminded the assembly that the topic for the day was sports.

"Yes, sir," said Ngess. "Here in Mungongoh, we work, eat, and sleep, and when we are not doing any of these, we simply remain idle. We never think of occupying ourselves in anything that we don't consider productive or useful. That is why, under king Awobua, we hardly ever had any forms of distraction, except when a few mangled dwarfs or miserable Mungongoh citizens were offered to the lions. Sports could change our lives a lot and transform some of the dullness into fun. On Earth sport is fun and a healthy practice. On Earth there are outdoor sports, indoor sports, team sports, in fact, hundreds of them."

"But we are different," said Funkuin. "Earthlings certainly need all these forms of distraction to take their minds off frivolous pursuits and curb the rampant crime rate. Out there, idleness is a breeding ground for crime, and an effective solution to the problem is to occupy much of their time."

"Yes," said a smartly dressed member of the AIDM. "Whoever introduced these forms of distraction to them did a wonderful thing. That was very thoughtful. But then Earthlings also use sports to keep fit and stay healthy. We don't need sports to stay healthy, do we? We have far longer lives, and our health is guaranteed by other things apart from sports."

"I beg to differ with you somehow," said Ngess. "In Mungongoh, most of us remained shapely because, unlike the members of the IRDI, we had no access to all that food and luxury. On the other hand, you can see how obese some of you privileged fellows turned out to be. Mobuh, his wife, and his kids were grossly overweight. And many of you here need to trim down considerably. That is one thing that physical sport does on Earth that can hardly be replaced simply by medicine. The earthlings are lucky that they have sports to rely on. I wonder how they came up with this great idea."

"Their God, or gods maybe, gave them sports for leisure, competition, and keeping fit," said Nyamfuka. "Best of all, it distracts them from idleness. Imagine what hideous misdemeanours the criminal minds of idle earthlings could develop and carry out if they all had a lot of time to spare."

"You are all right about the criminal nature of humans," said Ngess. "They somehow even manage to distort such a noble thing as sports to serve criminal purposes. Sports is now used everywhere on Earth for gambling."

There was general laughter.

"Is gambling that bad?" enquired Nange.

"Let's listen to Ngess," the king advised.

"Thank you, sir," said Ngess, humbly. "On Earth there are simple games of luck or clever brains that were created for leisure and passing time. You have chess, draughts, Monopoly, Scrabble, jigsaw puzzles, Dominos, you name them. These games are meant to be enjoyed by the players, and change to a broader form when they become publicly competitive. With competition, criminal minds have brought in the aspect of gambling. Now, on Earth there is virtually no game without this repugnant aspect attached to it. While gambling could be a source of fun and fortune, it is much more often a source of misfortune and crime. Earthlings have been known to fix games illegally, just to guarantee that they will win. Gambling has caused many to lose valuable property, their homes and wealth, and even their lives and the lives of others. Yes, gambling has resulted in bloody fights and much destruction."

"Phew," said a sombre looking woman. "Let us give up sports then."

"Not everything is bad and gloomy about it," replied Ngess. "Now that several aspects of sports involve competitive games, many earthlings have fun by simply watching or supporting one side or another. The players themselves come out with a lot of glory for themselves and their countries. You have the Olympics, national games, continental competitions, and world competitions."

"I say, Ngess," interrupted the queen. "Before being given the distinct position of chief minister, you were an ordinary citizen, with no access to earth monitors and earth scenes. You could only watch Mungongoh TV or listen to Mungongoh radio. How come you are so knowledgeable about Earth and virtually have a mastery of everything that occurs out there?"

"That, Madam, is thanks to the engineer Momjang."

The members of the newly created AIDM looked among themselves. There was no Momjang among them, and they were virtually the only ones who had access to TVs or radios that could capture scenes or radio programs from Earth.

"Not one of you, certainly," Ngess said. "To the members of the IRDI, I never meant anything, even though king Awobua always consulted me whenever your supposedly ingenious ideas went wrong. No! Momjang is the engineer whose squad installs all the communication facilities that all of you in this elite group use. He is in charge of their repairs and replacement. His workshop, therefore, has every device for monitoring Earth, and he is a close friend of mine. I have had much more access to happenings on Earth than most of you; and, although I am not a professor, I am certainly not a dull person. Momjang was quick to realize that my level of intelligence was certainly higher than that of many members of the IRDI."

Ngess was no longer the lowly Mungongoh citizen everybody knew. Apart from the king and queen, he was now the most senior and powerful person in Mungongoh. The king had not chosen him as chief minister for nothing. A lesser king than Fulumfuchong might have taken umbrage at his statement that he had all along been more intelligent than the members of the IRDI, a group to which he and his queen belonged. However, Fulumfuchong simply smiled and said, "Continue."

"Some games on Earth require much more physical exertion and are even more entertaining to both the players and the spectators. While most of these games require a ball of some sort, others such as swimming, sword play or fencing, and horseback riding are very entertaining and exciting. However, a ball is very important in most of their games. The swimmers use a ball for water polo, horse riders use a ball in polo, and balls are used in golf, football, basketball, handball, tennis, and so on."

"But what is in a ball?" asked the thickset professors.

"It is round, generally bounces, and rolls easily on any surface," explained Ngess. "That is why in ice hockey they don't need it - their flat object glides on the ice more smoothly. In badminton, the shuttle cock sails over the net and does not need to bounce or role. And the javelin and discus are shaped to suit the mode of throwing them."

"From what I have noticed, the balls are quite different, depending on the game," said Funkuin.

"They are different in materials and in size," Ngess said. "You have the small, light table tennis ball, the small, hard golf ball, the slightly bigger tennis ball, and then the bigger leather balls, and so on."

"In all these ball games, one hardly sees where the fun comes from," said the professor with the walrus moustache. "Imagine in baseball, a bloke throws the ball, another bloke hits it hard with a bat, and a third chap runs after it as it flies through the air in an attempt to catch it before it drops to the ground. Ridiculous."

"Or golf, where you place the ball on a tee and hit it with a club, walk to where it has dropped, and hit the ball across bunkers on to the green. Then you strive to send it into a hole," said a professor with white hair. "I wonder whether I could ever get any fun from that."

"The chaps on Earth certainly have too many games for their own good," another professor said.

"The games are there for several reasons," Ngess explained. "It could be for leisure, health, or entertainment. While some persons are interested in one sport, some are interested in others. In some cases, you may make a career in one or more of them."

"Maybe we should limit ourselves to football," proposed the youthful Nyamfuka. "Football could be quite interesting."

"That stupid game where people keep running after a leather ball and kicking it, often injuring one another?" said the white-haired professor. "I wonder what the earthlings see in it that makes them want to play and watch."

"That shows how totally ignorant you are about the ways of Earth when it concerns leisure and entertainment," said Nyamfuka. "Football is a source of leisure and excitement to many young men and even the elderly. In Africa, many boys shirk school and domestic work just to go and play football. Many sedentary, hard-working fellows keep healthy by playing football for exercise whenever possible. The uses and excitement of football do not end in the pitch. While millions of earthlings have their biggest exciting moments watching football, other millions earn a comfortable livelihood from it. Apart from professional footballers who make a fortune from it, there are contractors who earn huge sums from constructing and maintaining sports complexes, workers employed by various football associations, producers of footballs and football equipment, advertising companies, sports journalists, betting companies etc. I can assure you that football employs more than the population of Mungongoh."

"If it is like that," said the white head, "we should not bring it here. It should not be allowed in Mungongoh as it may completely divert us from our way of life."

"It is a good thing," argued Nyamfuka. "We could limit it to leisure and exercise though."

"What of the thousands of other games?" enquired Ngess. "What do you propose we do about them, or are you suggesting that only football is worth copying?"

"Certainly not," replied Nyamfuka. "We could consider handball, basketball, and tennis. Let's not forget that there are indoor games, too, such as chess, which we should copy for those who do not wish to exert themselves in any way."

"What is needed for all these?" asked the king. "From what I know, complex infrastructure will have to be put in place, for football especially."

"Not necessarily," replied Nyamfuka. "In our case, we can simplify everything."

"But it may mean bringing in many of those engineers from Earth to come and live among us during the construction period," Yivissi said.

"No!" said Ngess. "We would rather send our engineers out there to get the designs of their sports infrastructure. In technology, we are more advanced and smarter than them."

"I am still worried about this football issue," said Funkuin. "The earthlings often get so worked up about it that violence occurs. Now, watch."

She clicked on a button, and a football scene appeared on all the monitors in front of the members of the AIDM. The same scene came up on a monitor hanging from the ceiling not far from the throne, so the king and queen could watch comfortably. The scene that came up was quite ordinary. Cameroon was playing against France.

"Watch keenly," Funkuin announced.

Just then, two players jumped up to head the ball, and one of them furtively hit the other hard with his elbow before both of them landed on the ground. As both of them rolled around, apparently writhing in pain, it was not easy to make out what had happened. Another scene came up. The Cameroonian player wearing jersey number 9 was fouled as he rushed to score a goal. He was carried out on a stretcher with a broken leg. As the match continued, there were several acts of violence that culminated in a fight.

"As a result of one of these football matches on Earth," announced Funkuin, "two Latin American countries even went to war."

"In another case," she continued, after a brief pause, "an unfortunate player was shot dead by a disappointed fan. Some players have been known to drop dead in the football pitch."

"She is right," said the elderly female professor sitting next to her. "There is too much violence in this game. For all this while, we have been quite fine in Mungongoh without this horrid game. Why go and bring it here now?"

"When you get to know football, you will like the game," declared Nyamfuka. "As individuals or as a team, the glory in football stretches across the whole world. You are held in higher esteem than presidents and other renowned statesmen. We could even come out with a Mungongoh team that would compete in the world cup."

"What is the world cup?" asked a female.

"It is the greatest football jamboree on Earth. It comes up every four years," said Ngess.

"But we are not of Earth" said Funkuin. "We should not carry this diplomacy thing too far, only to find out when it is too late that we have become as decadent as the earthlings. You will soon say that we should go into boxing and wrestling. Have you ever watched a bout of American wrestling with those hunky fellows hammering at each other?"

"You have a point there," said Yivissi. "While in America, I watched a bout on TV where scantily dressed female wrestlers, divas they called them because of their beauty and shape, were tearing and screeching at each other in the ring."

"Let us decide on something," said the king, finally. "We are all aware of the importance of football on Earth, but we are equally aware of the negative sides of this game. We want fun, but we equally wish to live peaceful lives. We shall adopt football, but just for leisure and entertainment. There will be no professional footballers, no betting, and no adverts. Those who want to play will play, while those who simply want to watch will watch."

"But, sir," dared Ndaba, one of the youngest members of the AIDM. "Limiting football like that takes away all the fun and excitement in it. You need the drive and earnestness to win that comes from fanatical supporters. Supporters must throw their full weight behind their team."

Ndaba was one of the new members under observation that had been roped in to reinforce the team. He was a handsome young man whose knowledge of the earth was profound. His dissertation at the end of his university course had been entitled, 'The Earth, a playground for Mungongoh'. Ndaba was one of those Mungongoh persons who shared king Awobua's passion for Earth-watching. However, his reasons were different. What had actually attracted Ndaba to the Earth was football. As an alternate member of the IRDI, he had equally had access to interplanetary communications systems and audio visual services. Ndaba was about to be raised to the rank of a full member of the AIDM alongside Nange, a young female on whom he had an indescribable crush. After making his point about football, he turned and looked at her, expecting admiration and support. She obliged with a very charming smile.

"Sir," he continued, now certain that he was getting Nange's full attention, "to enjoy football fully we shall need to have teams and supporters. On earth you have school teams, neighbourhood teams, professional teams, and clubs. All of these have supporters and bring glory to whatever structure they represent through brilliant performance and victory. I tell you, football alone can take away all the dullness in Mungongoh and make life as electric as you can imagine."

"Are you suggesting that we adopt football and abandon all the other sports?" demanded Ngess. "Some of them could be more interesting, you know?"

"Yeah!" shouted one of the bald headed professors.

"Take table tennis for example, it is quite exciting and quite safe. The rough plays and dangers common in football do not obtain here."

"From the way earthlings are mad over it, there should be something in this football," said the king conclusively. "But I still think that we should be careful about the way it is practiced here. There shall be strict rules and great limitations to it."

"I wonder what those chaps on Earth see in football, running all over a pitch, exerting one's self to the limit, and sweating profusely." said Yivissi.

"Some earthlings even claim that it brings peace and friendship; but, if you watch a game of football, there is a lot of rough play, disputes between players, disputes between players and referees, disputes between coaches and referees, and in the end there are defeated sides that leave the football grounds very dejected and disappointed," said Funkuin. "Many players and supporters even cry miserably after losing a match. What sort of unity, friendship, and peace is that? I am sure I would be disappointed if women here take to football like some of those misguided females on Earth. We can play bridge, cards, scrabble, or chess. That is feminine enough for us."

"Talking about feminism," said Ngess. "On Earth, football is a man's thing. It is just that out on Earth now, women always want to do what men do. They call it emancipation."

"Yes, the Earth has changed," said Yivissi.

"Actually, it has changed quite a lot, madam!" said Ngess. "With your knowledge of Earth, you remember the period when men used to shoot at each other with pistols, or pierce each other with rapiers, just for the love of a woman and for gallantry. You remember, too, how Japanese fellows easily committed seppuku simply because they had been cuckolded?"

"Yes," said Yivissi, "and I believe very few men would be ready to do that now."

"Yes, madam, just as things have now changed, and women have started playing football. Try to imagine the possibility of one of those British ladies who never miss their tea time abandoning tea on a hot London afternoon and running and kicking footballs, possibly in her knickers and undergarments."

"That would have been unheard of," the queen said. "I agree with Professor Funkuin. Let the women stick to their Scrabble games and leave football to the men."

"That is alright with me," said Ndaba, "But on earth, many women do enjoy football as spectators. I hope ladies like Nange, who would certainly enjoy watching good football, will not be ridiculed by the others for participating in this kind of leisure."

"You have misunderstood me a little." said the queen. "For a woman to watch football does not mean she is going against the rules. I simply meant that women have better things to do than risk being hurt in a football pitch."

"We have virtually concluded on football," the king said. "I don't want us to consider rough games like American football and rugby. We have totally wiped out boxing and all forms of wrestling."

"What about swimming?" Nange asked "It is quite interesting to watch those trim men and women on Earth diving and swimming."

"That sport where they go splashing around stupidly in water?" asked one of the plump females.

"You need to see the way the earthlings enjoy themselves on some of those beaches - Cote d'Azure, Cancun, Mombasa, Limbe – it's really wonderful, I tell you," said Ndaba.

"But we don't have beaches here," said the old fellow. "You know very well that we don't have oceans and seas."

"We have lakes," said Nange stubbornly. "We could create a beach somewhere."

"We cannot tamper with our lakes," said Ngess "They are our sole source of fish and other marine products."

"We could create swimming pools then," said Ndaba, coming to the rescue of the woman he loved. "They have swimming pools on Earth, even in desert areas."

"That is true," said Nyamfuka whose knowledge of the Earth was deeper than most of the others. "We could easily construct a few swimming pools."

"What of the possibility of drowning?" demanded another old female academician. We know little or nothing about swimming."

"We could send instructors to Earth to learn. They will come back and teach those that are interested."

"Let us adopt it," said the king. "I think swimming is quite interesting."

He yawned. "I suppose we have had enough for today. We shall take another week and come back for the next item. What will it be?"

"Religion, sir," Ngess replied

"OK," said the king "We shall talk about religion during our next meeting."

4

A week passed, and the day for the next meeting came up.

"Shall we start, sir?" Ngess asked as the king and queen came in and sat down

"Go ahead," the king replied

"Another item that many earthlings are crazy about is religion," said Ngess.

"And what have we got to do with that?" asked one of the old eggheads.

"If it means something on Earth, then it could be very important," said Ngess.

"It is simply comprised of earthly beliefs. Of what use can religion be to us?" asked Funkuin.

At this point the king stepped in.

"I brought in this point," he said, "because of a few things I noticed on Earth. In many cases, religion has brought a lot of strife, discrimination, deceit and falsehood, cheating, and violence. On the other hand, religion is considered to have brought peace, development, and unity. As you see, it has many negative aspects, but I thought it may be of some advantage to us if we exploit only the good ones."

"I don't see how we can borrow something like that from the Earth and fit it into our context," said an old professor of history.

"Professor Buh knows what he is talking about," said Funkuin. "You see, although all the present religions on Earth claim to have divine origins, they all developed through the cultures of the earthlings. That is why in ancient times on Earth pagan polytheism was predominant as there was belief in several gods and other supernatural beings. The Greeks even thought that their gods were human-like in form and had emotions. They could protect and benefit people that paid them honour or did not offend them. These gods could have children, even with a human as the other parent. The gods could react in anger, just like any human, and mete out serious punishment to defaulting humans. Punishment could be in the form of defeat in war or some other catastrophe."

"Then we should forget about that at once," said an academic who had been concentrating seriously on what Funquin was saying. "We can't have gods that go after our wives and punish us in the bargain."

"Why did they need so many gods?" enquired a lady sitting next to Nange

"Each god had his or her role," replied Funkuin. "Their leader was Zeus, god of the sky, and his wife Hera was goddess of marriage. The other gods, too, had specific functions. These gods closely fitted into the history and beliefs of ancient Greece."

"What of the other ancient civilizations on Earth?" asked the youthful Ndaba.

"Ancient Rome had virtually the same gods as the Greeks, only they called them different names," explained Funkuin. "Zeus, the leader of the Greek gods, was called Jupiter by the Romans. Hera, the wife of Zeus and queen of the gods, was the Roman goddess Juno.

"Did all the ancient gods have human form?" asked Nange.

"Each civilization pictured its gods in their own way," said old professor Buh. "In ancient Greece and Rome, the belief in many mythical creatures with frightful shapes was common, but they gave the human shape to all their gods. Even Norse gods like Odin, father of the Norse gods, and Thor, the god of thunder, were generally human in form."

"Is that so?" asked the queen.

"Quite so," replied the professor. "As for Egyptian gods, they were often represented with human torsos but animal heads. Thoth, for example, had the head of an ibis while Mut had the head of a vulture. Other popular gods were Ra, who had the head of a hawk, Anubis, who had the head of a jackal, and Hathor, the goddess of love and laughter, who was given the head of a cow. The gods were also represented by symbols, such as the Sun disk."

"One lives and learns," said the queen.

"In some ancient religions on earth," Buh continued, "the gods were even represented by mythical creatures. For the Aztecs, Quetzalcoatl was believed to be a plumed serpent. The Maya went even further."

"Something worth noting is the importance of the sun in many of these ancient religions," said Funkuin. "That is why many divinities of ancient times on Earth were associated with the sun. The Inca, for example, believed the emperor was descended from the Sun god, Inti. The Aztecs worshipped Huitzilopochtli, the god of war and the Sun. Other civilizations before them worshipped the sun. In ancient Egypt, some of the most popular gods - Ra, Horus, and Khepri - were identified with the sun."

"All those jaw-breaking names are of no use to us now," said Nyamfuka. "We should not worry much about ancient gods when the earthlings themselves have discovered that they were all myths and now believe in one God."

"That is not true," said the old professor of history. "Hinduism, which is the third largest religion in the world after Christianity and Islam, accepts the presence of several gods: Brahmā, the creative spirit from which the universe arises; Vishnu, the force of order that sustains the universe;

and Shiva, the force that brings a cycle to an end, often identified with destruction."

"But Nyamfuka may be right," said Funkuin. "The Hindus also believe that all the deities you have mentioned above are embodied in one main deity, Saguna Brahman."

"We have spent too much time on ancient beliefs," said Ngess, who had not been too bothered about the ancient history of the Earth. It was for students of history to go into such frivolities. Although ancient history could be quite interesting, like what was unfolding now, there were many more important things to discuss. It was necessary to bring them round to recent things, and that was his forte. He was more versed in current things.

"Nyamfuka is right," Ngess continued, confidently. "Apart from some pockets of heathen beliefs in some remote corners of the earth where they still believe in many gods, the general trend is the belief in one God. On this, Christianity and Islam, the main religious options available, are conclusive. Each one claims to be the one and only true religion. And they are generally exclusionary, having the firm conviction that those who do not follow them are excluded from salvation. This way, members of the Islamic faith firmly believe that, as a follower of Mohamed, you cannot at the same time be a Christian, and Christians believe that you can only have salvation through Christ. Then, you have the Buddhists who believe in Buddha.

"Where are you heading to?" asked the king.

"Be patient, sir," said Ngess. "I will soon land. As we heard from Funkuin and the learned professor of history, most of the ancient religions on Earth are closely linked to the tradition and culture of the peoples involved. This same trend is reflected in the two greatest religions on Earth today. The Israelites and the Arabs lived side by side and evolved together. Their Religion and God have one source, linked to their history and culture in the ancient times. Now you have the followers of Buddha in South East Asia and China. Again linked to the cultures of the people in the area. On the other hand, we have never had a God in Mungongoh apart from our kings. Even when we were in Mars, there was no God. Which one are we going to worship now? If we want to follow the earthlings, we would have to pick up one of their religions and would be faced with a serious problem of choice. Should we become Christians, Mohammedans, or Buddhists?"

"Even in certain cultures on Earth" said the king, "it was believed, and is stilled believed in certain cases, that their monarchs or chiefs are gods or the incarnation of a god. I am now king here in Mungongoh where Awobua virtually had the status of a god. After the brief period that has passed, I have discovered that I am as ordinary as all of you. But then, as you have seen on Earth, almost all communities believe in a God or gods. The Red Indians, who roamed the lands of America long before usurpers came in from Europe, had Manitou. The ancient Greeks and Romans had Zeus and Jupiter. There were Norse gods, and each village in Africa had its gods. Even the Chukchi and Inuit had their gods. That is why I thought that there should be something in it. Now that we are borrowing certain ideas from the earth to complete our lives, why don't we borrow this one too?"

"The king may be right there," said Yivissi.

"May be right?" the king asked.

"I am sorry, dear," said Yivissi. "The king is right. There must be a good reason why all over the Earth people worship some god. Even ancient civilizations that were completely isolated from one another all worshipped gods or a God. We have equally noticed that religion brings peace, unity, and development. It has also made the lives of many women on earth worth living. Aging spinsters, to whom no man has proposed, or wives, whose errant husbands are always away from home, find much solace in attending extra church services, church meetings, choir practices, church excursions, you name them. Lonely wives, who would have strayed into the hands of other men, young girls torn between lust and respect for self and society, are kept on the straight and narrow path for fear of the wrath of God. I think Religion would help here in Mungongoh."

"You may have a point there," said Nyamfuka, "but don't forget that the fear of God can only obtain where the belief in the existence of God is well implanted. That is why God wields great power over the earthlings. Here, people have never believed in the existence of any powerful God, let alone one that would punish them for small transgressions. They will simply laugh it off."

"Don't be too sure about that," said one of the old female academicians. In the days of the Soviet Union, you remember that the government did everything to wipe out Religion from the minds of the people, but when the communist system collapsed, churches sprang up like mushrooms."

"Religion can be very addictive," said Yivissi, "and can easily be spread. Look at the heathens in Africa who received Christianity and Islam from invading Christian evangelists and Islamic horsemen on jihad, and are now even more fanatically loyal to Jesus or Mohamed."

"It may not be the same here," Nyamfuka insisted. "We have never believed in anything supernatural in Mungongoh, whereas on Earth, despite the fact that the European evangelists and Moslems called the African natives pagans, infidels, and heathens, the fellows had their own Religions all along, marked by superstitious beliefs in gods. It was, thus, easy for them to be swayed from one belief to the other. Superstition to an extent is the source of power for believers."

Ngess cleared his throat.

"If it were left to me, sir," he said looking at the king. "I'd rather keep religion out."

"But we are using the Earth as a source of inspiration for the new Mungongoh," said queen Yivissi, "and religion is one of those important aspects. We should, therefore, not abandon it just like that."

"The earthlings themselves are kind of confused about this religion thing," said Ngess. "Take Christianity, which is the most popular. There are many factions of it, and more keep surfacing. While most of them are convinced about the divinity of Jesus, others deny it. Because they believe the Christian doctrine of the Trinity to be incompatible with monotheism, some groups reject the idea of the holy trinity in favour of Unitarianism. Monotheism is a firm tenet of Muslims and Jews."

"There, you have just said it," said a grey haired female member of the AIDM. "While Christians are quite divided and openly condemn each other, Moslems are quite united. They all accept Mohamed as the greatest prophet and fervently believe in Allah."

"But it ends just there," replied Ngess. "When you watch news on earth TV stations, does it not occur to you that the division between Moslems could be greater? You have the moderates who believe that the fundamentalists and fanatics are straying off from true Islam. You also have a big chasm between the Sunnites and the Shiite. Sunnite suicide bombers do not spare any opportunity to wreak gory havoc on Shiite Moslems each time they have one of those elaborate ceremonies and processions. I tell you, the confusion is all over."

"I hadn't thought of that," said the grey-haired woman.

"This confusion starts with the Bible, a book that is supposed to show Christians the way, but which is rather full of bad examples exhibited by the ancients. There was a lot of sin as shown in the common history depicting the origin of Judaism. Lucifer sinned against God, and then Adam and Eve joined him to commit the next sin. It did not stop there. Great personalities like David and Solomon continued on the sinful path, a clear indication that earthlings will always easily succumb to temptation even in the presence of religion. On the other hand, during the existence of the Soviet Union where religion was considered as the opiate of the people, there was much more order and less crime, given the fact that citizens wanted to be upright in society. People were more worried about what society would say about their conduct than they were afraid of punishment from a God that easily forgives."

"You are beating about the bush," the king said.

"I am sorry, sir," replied Ngess. "Maybe I should use a few scenes from the earth to make my point better understood."

"Do," said the king yawning.

Ngess concentrated on the monitor in front of him for a short while, and an earth scene appeared on all the monitors in the room. The scene showed an old woman in an African village. She was one of those lucky old women whose children had somehow found their way to America and were now sending money to her regularly. She was expensively dressed and was reputed to regularly give a lot of money to the church. The scene opened with her stuffing money into her handbag to take to the priest to offer masses for the forgiveness of sins that her deceased husband might have committed on Earth. Just then, her neighbour rushed in pleading for assistance. His little child had fallen from a fruit tree and was badly hurt. The neighbour needed money in a hurry to rush the kid to the hospital. After listening impatiently to the desperate man's request to borrow money, she simply told him that she had not had a dime from anywhere for ages and advised him to look elsewhere. The scene continued with her moving to the church and handing over much money to the priest to say enough masses for the repose of the soul of her departed husband.

Ngess cleared his throat.

"In the former Soviet Union, this might not have happened. The old woman might have considered what society would say and helped her neighbour. In this case, she believes that the considerable sum given to the church will place her among those whom God has chosen."

Everybody smiled.

"Let's remain in Africa for a while," Ngess announced.

The scene moved to a family somewhere in the southern parts of Cameroon. Their daughter had brought in a Moslem from the North as her suitor. He was rejected outright. In fact, the girl's mother became hysterical.

The scenes kept changing. There was now a young man in front of a panel of interviewers selecting for a high profile job. When the predominantly Pentecostal jury discovered that the young man was of the Catholic Faith, his fate was sealed. He was rejected.

"We have seen quite enough to condemn religion already," said Ndaba.

"I am sure all of you must have seen enough to show you how religion has been transformed by fanatics into a very dangerous thing and is fast becoming a societal evil," Ngess said, looking round. "Just see what these demented fellows have made of it."

The next scene was somewhere in Guyana. A fellow called Jim Jones had rallied his followers into a clearing and distributed potassium cyanide for all to drink, claiming that their faith would protect them from the effects of the deadly poison. Everybody perished, of course.

"And there are many such fanatics out there," Ngess said. "Apart from such dangerous fellows, religion also comes with quacks and fake prophets. These smart guys make a comfortable living out of religion while their ignorant followers virtually adore them and spend millions on them."

The monitors brightened as a scene came up somewhere else in Africa. Elegantly dressed pastors who had parked posh cars outside the venue were spreading the word of God. Each one had a small topic that would have taken just about five minutes to exhaust, but each spoke for an hour. They put in a lot of colour and risked their vocal cords to breaking point.

After haranguing the huge crowds for several hours, it was time for 'deliverance' as they called it. Various persons stood up, supposedly with ailments, and declared how they had spent much money in vain to find a cure. Some claimed that they were possessed by evil spirits. A handful passed for cripples, while others gave the impression that they were blind. The pastors then came together and prayed over them, asking God to deliver them from the evil spirits that had taken over their bodies. The pastors then subsided into some gibberish. The people that were seeking deliverance seemed to have rehearsed their parts well. Only a trained eye would have realized that there was a lot of play- acting going on there.

The next act was what they termed 'testimonies'. A few actors came out and testified that they had earlier been relieved of incurable diseases or that demons had been cast out of their system. Everything was moving to a crescendo. The climax was really spectacular as the smiling pastors sat down and baskets went round for offertory. They were now confident that every member of the congregation would dive into his pockets or her hand bag and resurface with sums worth rewarding such big time play actors. They were earning their luxurious living.

"This misuse or misunderstanding of religion is not limited to Africa," Ngess said. "Watch."

The new scene was in Britain in a meeting of the top brass of the Anglican Church. While some traditionalists were protesting against considering female aspirants for positions of bishop, the moderates were insisting on the rights of women to aspire to that most honoured position. The argument was quite heated and almost went out of hand.

In another scene, Catholic Church officials were being pressured on one side by elderly ladies to issue hard sanctions against homosexual priests. On the other side, some priests were pointing out to them that the Anglicans were tolerating homosexuals to such a point that they were even being promoted to bishop.

"And religion in many cases has been accompanied by much violence," Ngess said.

The scene on the monitors switched to a place called Serbia. The carnage was beyond description. Thousands of persons were being massacred by the followers of Jesus, just because of their faith in Mohamed the prophet. Without saying more, Ngess switched to another scene. This time it was northern Nigeria. A band of Moslem youths were moving around like ferrets, sniffing out Christians, and taking away their miserable lives. The Moslem faithful were avenging the fact that some of the Christian infidels had dared to indulge in activities that were contrary to Islam.

"So far, we have been showing you the negative impacts of religion in more recent times," said Ngess, "but what about ancient times? Let Professor Funkuin and the historian tell us whether it was any better."

"This violence did not even spare the founder of the most popular religion called Christianity," Funkuin said. "Watch."

The scene was a place called Calvary. A young man called Jesus was nailed to a cross because of religious disagreements with Caiaphas and the Jewish priests. Viewing continued and many violent scenes depicting the persecution of the followers of Jesus passed through. It was clear that violence continued long after the crucifixion of Jesus. This was intensified and countered by scenes of valiant young men in their prime who left England and Europe to go on crusades or holy wars around Jerusalem. Many were killed in these useless wars or came back old and tired.

"I will stop here," said Funkuin, "and let Professor Buh continue with even more ancient times on Earth.

"In ancient times," said Buh, the learned professor of history, "religious practice was worse and often outright cruel. Let's consider some of the ancient civilizations. In pre-Columbian times among the Inca, Aztec, and Maya, religious practices involved rituals often characterized by blood sacrifice. The Aztec, for example, believed that many gods required human support and could weaken or die if people did not sustain them by means of sacrifices. Human sacrifices were the main source of this gory nourishment for gods, and some of it was self-sacrifice. The Maya, for example, often practiced self-mutilation for the purpose of shedding blood during rituals. This is possibly why they revered Ixtab, goddess of suicide. Aztec warriors sometimes opted to be killed during the more important sacrificial rituals."

"It would have been better," said Funkuin, "if they had stuck to self-mutilation. But the Inca and Aztecs indulged more in sacrificing others, and this meant ritualistic killing. The Maya also went into this occasionally. Victims of sacrifice could be citizens or even children, depending on the tastes of the god. Often, prisoners of war were used. It is believed that on one occasion during an Aztec sacrificial ritual, more than 10,000 captives were sacrificed."

Ngess took over and continued.

"As you all see, religion may have its good side, but this is sadly eclipsed by the repugnant or abusive use of it by individuals. I advise we continue living as before without bringing in religion to disturb our lives."

"With all due respect, sir," said Nange, "don't you think you are exaggerating a bit? From your presentation, one can only conclude that religion has no good side to it and is totally a terrible thing."

"Isn't it?" asked Ngess. "Okay, watch."

A series of very violent earth scenes came up. Suicide bombers were blowing themselves to shreds and taking down with them hundreds of innocent people. It continued to a climax where two of the tallest buildings in the world were brought down to rubble by terrorists, and this shocking disaster took away the lives of many.

"That is religion for you," said Ngess. "These attacks were not staged by nationalists or revolutionaries. None of them would have imagined such a big thing. This is the work of religious extremists or fundamentalists."

"Why don't we look at the other side of religion?" asked Nange, taking over control of the monitors. "Watch these scenes."

She started with a picture depicting the Islamic Bank.

"This bank," she said, "is Islamic and religious and its contribution to developmental issues such as health, education, agriculture, employment etc. is immense."

The scenes kept changing and moved through several locations in Africa where doctors and reverend sisters were working in hospitals, taking care of the sick. There equally leper settlements and centres for people with special needs run by different religious denominations.

"These may look like regular health institutions, but they would never have been there to help the people if religious denominations did not bring them," Nange explained.

The next scene started from Sasse College in Buea, a town in Cameroon, and went through several schools ranging from primary to high schools set up by various religious denominations.

"In most of these countries, many people would never have had a chance to receive an education if these schools did not exist."

"That does not hold here in our context," said Nyamfuka. "We have all the schools and health facilities we need."

"The idea here is simply to show you that religion has its positive side. It may occur here in other forms. Just as all the negative things about religion happening on Earth may not occur here."

"Anything more?" the king asked.

"Yes, sir," Nange replied, switching to other scenes.

The Pope was touring some countries of the world, pulling mammoth crowds.

"That shows how popular religion is on Earth," said Nange.

In other scenes, evangelists were talking to huge crowds.

Then there was this scene on doctrine classes where children were groomed on how to live respectable lives based on religion and the fear of God. Even some married couples were receiving doctrine.

Nange stopped to explain.

"As you see here the rate of divorce is going overboard in areas where the value of religion has dropped. God fearing people out there have learnt how to tolerate and live throughout their lives with their spouses no matter how adverse the condition becomes," she said.

"There is something in that," said the queen. "I think we should consider religion."

"Maybe," said Ngess. "But we should choose just one. Religious conflicts on Earth mainly stem from the fact that there are many religions competing with one another. And then there is so much tolerance that charlatans and business men have transformed religion into a business venture. There are thousands of denominations today on Earth, and the number keeps increasing rapidly. It is very lucrative business, you know."

"Yes," agreed the king. "We should adopt some form of religion. No fanatics, no digressions. The floor is open. Let us choose something."

"I suppose that we abandon all the contemporary religions on Earth and borrow from ancient Rome and Greece," said Nyamfuka. "Instead of an abstract being whose real name, face, gender, or age we don't know. Let us have gods like Zeus, Hera, Aphrodite, and others."

"No!" said Funkuin. "The Greek and Roman gods displayed a lot of lust for things of the flesh, unbridled jealousy, and a taste for vengeance. They were known to be arbitrary in many cases."

"That's quite right," said Buh, the professor of history. "The gods of ancient Greece and Rome were often involved in one form of scheming or another. The Trojan War lasted for ten years because the gods kept taking sides. Zeus, the head god, was always involved in escapades with one earthly female or another, keeping his wife Hera constantly on her feet in a bid to control her errant husband. We cannot have that kind of religion here."

"I admire the Buddhists. Those lamas seem to be very devoted and live very humble lives," said one of the bald academicians.

"And have an earthling for our god?" asked Funkuin. "The Dalai Lama, the present incarnation of Buddha, is a Tibetan Lama."

"Let us try Islam then?" proposed Nyamfuka. "This is one religion we can rely on."

"There we might need to take turns in going on pilgrimage to Mecca each year," said Ndaba.

"No problem," replied Nyamfuka. "We can always arrange that."

"Wait a minute," said Funkin. "You guys seem to be talking conclusively, forgetting about the fact that we, the women, may have several objections here. From my knowledge of Islam, the man has a certain advantage over the woman."

"What do you mean?" asked Nange.

"The men go where they want while the women are obliged to live restricted lives and cover their faces with a veil," said Funkuin. "In the case of adultery, the woman risks being stoned to death while the man may take as many as four wives."

"Four wives?" all the female academicians shouted.

"Yes, and there are lots of other things to worry about."

48

"Let's drop it," said Yivissi the queen. "It should be noted that we the women are opposed to it."

"That is alright, my dear," the king said. "Let us look at Christianity and see what we can make of it."

"Christianity may be too broad," said Ngess. "The followers of Christ have undergone so much splintering that some have become antichrists."

"From the arguments and proposals put forward so far, it is clear that most of you have a very limited scope when it comes to religious aspects on Earth," Dr. Kini said. "If we leave out the old religions that have been jettisoned by the earthlings themselves, we realize that religion has virtually narrowed to one. What I mean is that virtually all of them believe in one God and the notion of gods no longer exists. The Jesus the Catholics consider as God - and at the same time the son of God - may not be accepted by all, but the God in whom the Catholics believe is the same God revered by Moslems. The Muslims may call him Allah; others may call him Jehovah or Yahweh. As earlier pointed out by professor Buh, the Incas had RasCapac, the Egyptians had Ra and others, and there were gods like Thor. The Aborigines in Australia, the Africans, and other peoples had their gods, although Europeans considered them as heathen. But then this great God also known as Allah came in and defeated all of them. All these other gods were pushed out through Christian evangelization and crusades, and Muslim Jihads, and now virtually the whole earth believes in this God. This shows that he is great indeed. What we want is a God in whom we will believe. Let us adopt this God and eliminate the negative aspects."

"What of those talismans that the Catholics use, do we adopt those too?" asked Nyamfuka.

"What talismans?" enquired Nange. "The Catholics don't believe in idols and things like that. It is the heathens that use them."

"But the Catholics do," insisted Nyamfuka. "They hang things around their necks and at times around their waists, and some of them believe in the power of some object they call a rosary."

"Those are mere prayer tools," said Ngess. "They pray only to their God and not to the items mentioned by Nyamfuka."

"Why would they need things like that?" asked Ndaba.

"The problem with many Christian churches now is that there is too much superstition," said Ngess. "Heathen beliefs were condemned and abandoned because they were full of superstition. You cannot wear an object around your neck or waist or any part of your body and think that it can protect you against danger or evil or bring you luck. Some Christians even believe that they can succeed in getting absolution for crimes committed by deceased ancestors. That is why I said we should forget about religion."

"There is this interesting religion called Baha'i. Its origin is Iranian, and it was founded by Baha'u'llah in the middle of the 19th century," said Funkuin. "Its central tenets are the unity of all religions and the unity of all humankind. There are no rituals and no priesthood. Its believers reject superficial differences, such as caste or class, between people. The religion has just above 5 million adherents but I think it is worth trying it."

"That sounds like what we want," said Ndaba. "But if it still has so few followers on earth, then there might be something wrong with it."

"Okay," said the king. "We shall put it to vote. This time, it will be quite free and fair. No intimidating Professor Itoff to compel us to vote for what he stands for."

Voting was rapid and the majority voted against the bringing in of a religion of any type.

The meeting was adjourned for another week.

5

The meeting resumed as scheduled in a week's time.

"Let us move to the next item," said Ngess. "Culture and Arts."

"I think I can speak authoritatively here," said Funkuin. "After taking over from Itoff and switching over to History, I thoroughly went through all the archives of Professor Itoff. I discovered lots of things that he knew that were kept hidden from all of us."

"That is criminal," said Yivissi.

"Maybe he had his reasons," said Funkuin.

"What did you discover?" asked the king.

"As all of you know," said Funkuin, "the culture of a people is closely linked with the history of the land. We have our history, our music, our language, our diet, our forms of dressing, and other items. On the other hand, cultures are dying on Earth, replaced by decadent music, cinema, and dances full of sexual expressions. While researching into the archives of Itoff, I discovered that one or two of our space craft never got to land in Mungongoh after we left Mars. Further research showed that they might have landed somewhere on earth. I did a thorough study of all the peoples of Earth and finally came across a tribe in a small country, Cameroon, called Kom. Their language is very similar to ours and they dress with dallas like us, only this honourable dress is being abandoned out there in favour of fashion from other parts of the world. Watch!"

The monitor came on with a scene in the Kom palace. There, the traditional ruler, or Fon, was presiding over a traditional occasion. The Fon was dressed in a beautiful dalla, and his courtiers were equally well dressed. A few of them dressed in western style clothing. Some women were dancing gracefully and singing beautifully.

"That is the Fumbang dance," informed Funkuin. "There is very beautiful singing there, but listen to the language."

She allowed the scene to continue till the end as everybody present was enjoying the dancing. Then the women were replaced by some active masked youths dressed in sack cloth covered with feathers, with some noisy rattles tied around their ankles.

"The people call this Mukum," Funkuin announced. "They dance to the tune of drums and xylophones."

"The language is very much like ours," said Nange. "But they could not have come from Mungongoh. They all have some kind of coffee brown colour."

"That," said Funkuin "is probably because they landed in the tropics, were exposed to the scorching sun, and were slowly baked into that nice attractive colour."

"This is difficult to believe," said Yivissi. "This issue of complete transformation into blacks, I just can't figure it out."

"We are talking about something that occurred a few hundred thousand years ago. The people certainly did not go straight to this place. They probably strayed around for quite a long while. Whatever the case, they have been living in this place for ages. That is clearly our language and our form of dressing."

"What I admire most is that dancing," said Ndaba. "The women were great, and what graceful steps. The masquerades, too, were wonderful. Where would they have learnt that?"

"They developed alongside other tribes of the area, who copied the dalla from them, but from whom they also copied much," said Funkuin. "However, my point here is that in terms of culture, we should copy things like those beautiful but harmless traditional dances."

"On earth, the history and culture of a people is always linked with some kind of belief or religion," said Ngess. "They even swear by the gods or symbols of their belief. What else have you noticed about this people Professor Funkuin?"

"You have a good point there," Funkuin replied. "The history of ancient Rome, for example, was tied to belief in their gods at that time, and they easily swore by Jupiter or by Juno while the Norsemen swore by Thor. From a close study of these Kom people, I noticed that the men swore by Kwifoin - some god of theirs I suppose. Thousands of years on Earth certainly linked them closely with the other peoples of the area, from whom they probably adopted this belief. I later on discovered that most of the tribes around them swore by Kwifoin, which up till now has been believed to be the guiding force of each tribe."

"Here on Mungongoh," said Ngess, "we don't swear. We neither plead with nor thank any super-being for good things, like the Christians on Earth always thank God. Here we know only our king, and now we have the luck to have a kind, understanding, and generous one."

"Let's copy the good cultural aspects as Professor Funkuin said," said the king. "No frivolous dances, dresses, films etc."

"There is one good element of culture that the ancient Greeks had, and that is being copied by other countries on earth, though very slowly and at times with much resistance from reactionary regimes," said Ndaba.

"And what is that?" asked the king.

"Democracy, sir," Ndaba answered.

"Democracy?" asked Funkuin. "But that infringes upon the powers of the king."

"Yes," offered Nyamfuka. "Democracy often comes with parliaments, which make all the decisions. The king becomes a mere figure head."

"How many of us are sitting here around this table?" Ngess asked.

"Why, we are fifty one," replied Nange.

"That is," said Ngess, "fifty members of the AIDM and me, the chief adviser, right?"

"Quite right," replied Nange.

"And what else are we doing here?" continued Ngess. "We are all discussing things concerning Mungongoh and proposing ideas to the king to enable him make positive decisions. Besides, the king has other advisers. In short with all the talk about democracy on Earth, I wonder if any country really practices it the way it should be done."

"What of Britain and America?" asked Yivissi.

"The representatives of the people in parliament or congress, the senate or house of lords, are mostly rich privileged people who know very little about the problems and aspirations of the masses," said Ngess. "They are there to enrich themselves, work for their own class, which is composed of the rich, defend the policies of the government if they are of the governing party, or condemn every act of the government if they are in the opposition. On the other hand, here we have not been voted in by anybody, but we truly represent the aspirations of all the people of Mungongoh."

"Well said," shouted the queen, clapping. "What we need from the Earth are things that can improve our lives. We don't need to bring in anything just because it is talked about or practiced on Earth."

"Your highness," said Ngess, "when Professor Funkuin spoke, she mentioned the importance of history. Today in Mungongoh, the common man only knows that we came from Mars and have lived in Mungongoh for ages. Only historians like Professor Funkuin know certain details. Now it turns out that Itoff had been hiding some important information. We don't know how many wars we have fought on this planet and against whom. We also need to know whether the Earth is the first planet that we have ever had access to and so on."

"So, what should we do about that?" asked the king.

"Improve the research into our history and make all information known," replied Ngess.

"That is fine," said the king.

He turned to the queen. "My dear, you remember we went to the theatre a few times when we were on Earth?"

"Yes, I remember," the queen replied. "We watched ballets on a few occasions, and then circus acts and other forms of entertainment all performed with dexterity and expert mastery. I think we should introduce that here."

"As Ngess mentioned earlier, our lives have mainly been work or just existing," said the king. "We have hardly ever been bothered about entertainment, especially as the little that was offered was gruesome. Yes, the spectacle of lions eating dwarfs and condemned Mungongoh citizens was so repulsive that only sadists could enjoy it. We should really consider interesting aspects that could considerably brighten up our lives."

"Really, we should brighten up our lives as the king said," said Funkuin. "We have looked at sports and borrowed a few aspects. We have dismissed religion completely. Now we are working on culture and have identified some dances. We need to move ahead, but what concretely do we consider next?"

"I suggest we start by identifying what we would enjoy best," proposed Ndaba. "Why don't we start with ballet, where those beautiful girls move lithely on the tips of their toes, then the svelte young men pick them up, sniff at them, and put them back down each time?"

"How many persons here can dance ballet?" asked Funkuin. "And the steps are so complicated."

"We could bring them in from the earth to display," said the king.

"The opera will be easier for us to handle ourselves and entertain our folk," said Nange. "After all, it is just singing and acting."

"Opera?" exclaimed Nyamfuka. "That is a crazy thing to propose. Imagine how people take years to transform angelic voices into shrieks and croaks. I don't believe anybody in Mungongoh would be interested in that."

"There is the circus, too," Yivissi said. "I watched it a few times while on earth. Athletic boys and girls swing on trapezes. And there are animals of all sorts, not just your crazy lions."

"To think of animals," said Nyamfuka, "why don't we set up a zoo?"

"We should look at more practical things first," said Ngess. "A zoo may come with complications, acclimatization, feeding, veterinary care, and so forth."

"But all the other things already mentioned are not yet feasible here. We have to build theatre houses and train performers. That will not be easy," said Nyamfuka.

"We could consider the other option of importing performers from the Earth as the king already proposed," said Ngess. "They are quite experienced and even build their own makeshift theatres when they are ambulant."

"I don't trust the earthlings," said the cross-eyed academician. "Bring in troupes of them, and our young men and women are in trouble."

"But we have already agreed that earthlings will have very short stays here. We will watch them closely. They come, perform, and leave," said Ngess.

"That is more comforting," the woman replied.

"That is okay," said the king. "Now, let's adjourn for today and fix our next meeting for next week. Could we know what shall come next?"

"This next point is quite important, sir," replied Ngess. "It concerns our dwarfs."

6

The next meeting came up as expected. The king welcomed everybody to his palace and handed over to Ngess and Funkuin.

Ngess stood up, welcomed everybody, and continued.

"We are now talking about the dwarfs, their status in society, and how we should coexist with them." He turned to Funkuin. "What do you have to say Professor?"

"When our fore parents landed on Mungongoh," explained Funkuin, the doctor of hate sciences now become professor of history, "the dwarfs had the planet to themselves. They called this planet Jvatein and called themselves Mungongli. They roamed this place freely until our ancestors came in and easily subdued them, thanks to our higher intellect. However, our ancestors never thought of staying long here as their ultimate target was some other nice place like the Earth. They, therefore, did not give much thought to the dwarfs and simply went ahead to transform those they could lay hands on into servers. The rest of the dwarfs ended up underground and will never forgive us for taking away their land. Their present leader, Fuam, would seize the slightest opportunity to rise against us. Fuam and her horde of rebel dwarfs actually call us Ikwi and hate the name Mungongoh on the basis that it is a name imposed by the usurpers of their land. "

"From this historical background," said Ngess, "we all see that the dwarf problem is quite serious and has to be handled with care. During the reign of previous monarchs, a few uprisings occurred, although the dwarfs were easily overpowered. During the reign of Awobua and the few kings before him, no uprisings were registered. Rather, dwarfs were considered as of no consequence and no thought was given to them. Our ideas about dwarfs were limited to the ones that served us and the thieving habits of the others. From Professor Funkuin's exposé, we are now all aware of the problem simmering beneath our feet, orchestrated by Fuam. We have always minimized this threat, but one day it may boil over."

"I think you are taking the thing too far," said the king. "We did not come here to discuss some dismal rebel dwarfs. I am sure what we came here to discuss was the status of the dwarfs and how we should treat them, and I suppose this concerns the dwarfs living with us and serving us, not the handful of wild dwarfs living underground in caves."

"I would not call the rebel dwarfs a handful, sir," replied Ngess. "I suspect they may even be more than us in population. It is just that somehow our surveillance systems cannot penetrate into their underground abodes, and we cannot watch them the way we watch happenings on earth. I still believe in caution."

Ngess turned from the king and concentrated on the rest of the assembly.

"We are all aware of the number of dwarfs eaten by Awobua's lions," he said. "We are aware of the menial role of dwarfs up until now, and the fact that we have always considered them lesser beings. We are equally aware of the fact that the dwarfs are the true owners of Mungongoh. There are, therefore, grounds for discontent on their part."

"We conquered the dwarfs and took over Mungongoh from them," said an old bloke with a huge skull. "We are now the true owners of Mungongoh and no dwarf can raise a finger."

"And dwarfs are very unreliable and rascally," said another member of the AIDM.

"They pilfer whatever we leave lying around our homes that is not nailed down," said one of the hawkish female academicians. "I am sure, if we searched their underground abodes, we would find lots of stolen items."

"I may be mistaken," said Nange, "but I think that dwarfs are in their place, and we don't need to worry about them."

"I disagree with that," said Nyamfuka. "We still have to consider the position of the dwarf in Mungongoh. They have a considerable population, and we are condemned to live with them forever. They have been very useful to us despite their bad habits. We either consider dwarfs as almost our equals or as completely lesser beings. If we consider them equals, they should equally have access to education and aspire to high positions. Otherwise, they maintain their position of servants and underdogs."

"Nyamfuka has spoken intelligently and brought out all the options," the king said. "Truly the dwarfs are useful, and we cannot do without them. I will keep my palace dwarfs. I enjoy their services, and we will continue selecting them from the best."

"However," said the queen, "they shall be well-treated. No more harassment and the dreadful prospect of ending up walloped by lions. We shall equally improve upon their living quarters."

"I see you have even provided stools for them, sir," said Funkuin.

"Yes," replied Yivissi. "They also deserve to be well-treated. The little fellows are quite useful and can be very entertaining at times."

"The question now," said Ngess, "is whether we should treat them almost as equals."

"That cannot be," protested four of the old female academicians.

"I can't see myself being treated as a dwarf," continued one of them.

"There you are mistaken," said Ngess. "We mean giving dwarfs almost the same privileges that you have as a citizen of Mungongoh."

"Dwarfs will always be dwarfs," she replied indignantly. "Very soon you will say that our young men could get married to those stunted females."

"I have always wondered how it would be like to make love to a dwarf woman," Ndaba joked.

"You wouldn't step that low, would you?" Nange asked sternly. "You are not satisfied with all the beautiful Mungongoh females that you can choose from?"

"Don't panic," laughed Nyamfuka. "Ndaba's love and admiration for you is very evident, and I am sure no dwarf belle is beautiful enough to threaten your place in his heart."

There was general laughter.

"This is not a laughing matter," said Funkuin sternly. "Marrying dwarfs or even having an affair with them is criminal," she continued, looking warningly at Nyamfuka. "In no way can we allow them to become our equals. We shall treat them fairly but no more. You can't expect dwarfs to do anything but menial jobs."

"In that case," said Yivissi, "we should all accept that they will not be treated simply as serfs but will be fairly rewarded for their menial jobs."

"That is it," agreed Nange and Ndaba together.

"That is not it," said another group of academicians.

"Let's take over this discussion about our dwarfs again," the king said. "We need to agree somehow about their future status."

"Those nasty fellows," grumbled one cross-eyed female. "Why should we bother about those snatchers? They pick

64

clothes off our drying line, pilfer our food, and sneak away anything they can lay their filthy paws on."

She had some supporters.

"Let us forget about the dwarfs," the thickset professor said.

"We can't leave out the dwarfs," Ngess said. "Don't forget that our forefathers met them here when they arrived. Mungongoh is actually their home."

"They have been our servants ever since," said the white haired professor. "It should remain that way. We still need them to do our menial jobs."

"If you need them," said Ngess, "then you need them to survive. Improve upon their welfare."

"That is true," said Nyamfuka. "With the new Mungongoh, we need them to do not only the menial work but also the extra crude labour."

"What extra work is that?" asked Nange.

"Our main form of payment for services that we shall consume from earthlings in this new dispensation shall be in the form of our minerals, such as the one the greedy earthlings call gold, and precious stones," said Nyamfuka. "We would need some crude labour to extract these from rocks. On Earth extracting precious stones involves a lot of work, and they often have to dig quite deep before they extract significant quantities. Here in Mungongoh, it might not be that tedious, but we shall still need a lot of crude labour, especially when we are through with the ones on the surface. Here our little men will come in very handy. I suggest we treat them better than Awobua and use them to make a fortune for Mungngoh."

"Talking about dwarfs," said Yivissi. "I still think we should change their lifestyle, give them education, and improve upon their living standards."

"How?" asked the cross-eyed female who had spoken earlier against the dwarfs. "You would soon suggest, your highness, that we should make dwarfs Mungongoh citizens."

"That is a great idea," said Yivissi. "Thank you for bringing it up. I suggest we take that proposal of hers seriously."

The cross-eyed female was confused.

"Well, madam," said Ngess respectfully. "It is quite a delicate issue. We can't just make dwarfs Mungongoh citizens. The situation needs a lot of looking into and consideration. All we can do for now is make their situation better."

"Can we at least bring them out of the caves and give them some decent lives?" the soft hearted Yivissi asked.

"No! That is not possible, dear," the king said firmly. "There are limits to certain things."

"The king is right," said Ngess. "Before our forefathers got here, the dwarfs were roaming freely on this land. We occupied the place by force, and the dwarfs retreated to the caves. Since then they have been sizzling for revenge. We have so far succeeded in subduing them because of our more advanced technology. But then, we have always taken advantage of the fact that they have chosen to remain underground. We prefer them away from our streets, apart from those who work for us."

"We also have to think of something else," said Nyamfuka. "You can only bring the dwarfs out from the caves by force, and that means war. I am not sure the short, stout fellows will be willing to come out of their caves and live among us. The same way we are scared of living together with them, so are they strongly against socializing with us. I tell you, they loath us the way this earthling gladiator they called Spartacus loathed his owners. If we try to force them

66

out of their caves, there will likely be serious war. In such a case, the fighting will mostly be around the caves. Many of you may not be aware of the catacombs on Earth, such as the ones in Odessa and Paris. This is a complicated network of underground rooms and passages, and that is just how the caves of our dwarfs are."

"We don't want any confrontation with the dwarfs," the king said. "So we can't force them to come out. Let us be contented with making them happier with us."

"We should at least make the killing of a dwarf a criminal act," said Yivissi.

"There," replied a member of the AIDM. "We are not Awobua, who kept hammering on them with brute force. On the other hand, publicly declaring the killing of a dwarf a crime gives the impression that they are equal to us. Dwarfs are things that can be disposed of if we have to or if we consider so."

Ngess cleared his throat, "What do you say Professor Funkuin?"

Although the king, queen, and Ngess were present, Funkuin was the official head of the AIDM.

"Having listened keenly to the discussions," said Funkuin, "I am of the opinion that we should treat the dwarfs well, give them the impression that they are better off with us than the dreaded Awubua, and then use them as beasts of burden when the time comes. That way, they will do all that we want without complaining. I think it is better for the dwarfs to stay in their caves, and only those who work for us should be provided with living quarters. For this other extraction work, they will only come out to work and go back to their caves. During work, they shall be closely watched, and after work we will not have the problem of hobnobbing all over the place with dwarfs. Meanwhile, we would have taken all the discontent from the dwarfs and kept them busy. A combination of idleness and discontent is quite dangerous and is often the root of revolutions."

The king started clapping and was followed by the rest of the top brains of Mungongoh, with Nyamfuka clapping most vigorously.

"From the applause," said Ngess, "it is evident that her proposal is an excellent one, accepted by all. It shows that the king was most appropriate in his choice of Professor Funkuin as head of the AIDM."

"I suppose we have come to the end of the first meeting of the AIDM," the king said conclusively. "Yivissi, Ngess, and I were simply present to lay the foundation. Further meetings will continue under Professor Funkuin whenever she calls them. Ngess may attend or preside once in a while, depending on the circumstances or importance of the meeting. For now, Ngess shall work out the details on what we have all agreed on."

"The king took a sip from his cup of Kola coffee. This was a lot better than Mukal," he thought.

"The palace shall be a merry place," he continued. "You all remember the solitary arrangement that Awobua preferred. The whole of Mungongoh shall be transformed into a lively planet, admired by all the earthly nations with whom we will establish relationships."

The decisions adopted in this important meeting, with details developed by committees, were immediately implemented. Mungongoh became a bee hive of activity, as plans for playgrounds, theatres, and other infrastructure were developed. A school of diplomacy was programmed to be incorporated in the University of Mungongoh, where diplomats would be trained on how to handle earthlings expertly.

7

Deep in the bowels of Mungongoh, a strange meeting was going on. Fuam, the leader of the rebel dwarfs, had assembled dwarf leaders to assess the new king of Mungongoh, the relationship between the new Mungongoh and the dwarfs, and the way forward. According to Fuam, they had been docile for too long and could not remain so while there was so much bustle and activity in Mungongoh. The meeting was attended by all the rebel dwarf leaders from near and far.

The venue was an old Ayissi, a large meeting place that normally served as a kind of bar to the dwarfs. Ayissis were large underground halls carved out of rocks and located at strategic junctions in the underground network of tunnels. These large, low underground halls were furnished with crude benches and tables hewn from stone. Like the various tunnels that led to dwellings and other parts of the underground world of the dwarfs, the Ayissis were lit by some rock that gave out enough light to make everyplace as bright as day.

The diminutive fellows always gathered in such places to consume an alcoholic brew produced from fermented mushrooms. Their drinking mugs were also of stone, and each dwarf had one and carried it to every drinking bout. In the Ayissis, there were no barmen. Each reveller made and brought his or her brew. When consuming this drink they called ntop, the revellers generally exchanged jokes and information about their escapades with Mungongoh citizens.

Dwarfs never invested in anything and, thus, had very little property. Each dwarf made his or her own clothes and the few household items that they owned. The rest of their items were pilfered from Mungongoh citizens. The dwarfs lived very simple lives, did not bother themselves with education, did not care for things like hospitals, and had no games. A dwarf's life was comprised of eating, sleeping, drinking ntop in one of the Ayissis, and making a lot of noise. These drinking bouts were often accompanied by brawls sparked by the least provocation.

The venue for this meeting was the largest Ayissi in the dwarf world; all Fuam's meetings were organized here. The dwarf leaders then took the message and organized other meetings in the various Ayissis in their areas. That way, information circulated thoroughly. On this occasion, every dwarf was quiet and attentive as Fuam stood on a crude table to open the meeting.

"Fellow Mungongli," she said, "all of you are welcomed in this Ayissi. Many of you have left your Ayissis in far off areas to come to this one because of this most serious occasion. I will, thus, expect all of you to stay calm and attentive, put away your mugs of ntop, and participate fully in this most important meeting."

Fuam paused as tremendous applause came from the gathering of the dwarfs. The dwarfs were not used to clapping. When they were excited or thought that some speech or act needed to be applauded, they simply made a strange noise, just like the whinnying of a horse. After smiling appreciatively for a while, she raised her right hand in a bid to stop the continuing applause.

"The terrible Awobua is now gone. Many dwarfs lost their lives at the hands of this tyrant. The status of the dwarfs was brought down to dust, and we were like mud during his reign. But all tyranny must have an end, and his end came."

She was forced to pause again because of another tremendous applause of the strange noise.

"They now have a new king, Fulumfuchong," she continued. "One Mungongoh king has gone and another one has replaced him. Now, tell me what the difference is."

"You may say that this one is more humane and that the dwarfs stand less chances of dying in his hands, but are we better off?"

Fuam looked round the assembly of dwarfs. Finally, her gaze concentrated on a stout fellow who looked much neater and cleaner than the rest of the crowd.

"Much has been going on in the palace up there for the past weeks, and we need to know everything and take our own decision down here. Kanjam is one of the attendants in the palace and has used his sharp brain to record every discussion and activity that has been going on out there. We will listen to him, ask any question, and then decide what to do next. Let us be attentive."

Kanjam stood up smiling, cleared his throat, and rubbed his prominent stomach.

"Fellow Mungongli," he said, "I greet you all. I am a head attendant at the royal palace of Mungongoh and one of the survivors of the bloody reign of King Awobua. When he was there, a dwarf's life was never certain. Awobua could pound you to death simply to assuage some baseless anger. Now he is gone and King Fulumfuchong promises to be a better person. Mind you, there is no good person in Mungongoh when it concerns us Mungongli. Anyway, what is new is that the IRDI has been transformed into the AIDM. It may not mean anything to us, but the simple understanding is that Munongo will change from its intention of crushing the Earth to the option of collaborating with it. You may soon find earthlings visiting on regular basis. The king has equally appointed new top officials. You all remember that Mobuh and Itoff were torn to shreds by lions alongside their king.

For the past weeks, the king and his new top counsellors, who form the AIDM, have been working on what they want the new Mungongoh to be. I want to state here that the Mungongli were an item on the agenda. This item was not put there for our own good, however. They simply want to see how they can make best use of Mungongli without destroying them the way Awobua was doing. Yes, my brothers and sisters, they want to use us to do work that none of them would touch. This new work would be even rougher and more tedious than the menial jobs we do in the palace and in some big institutions. With this new work, they will need lots of Mungongli labour and will come after all of you down here."

Kanjam rubbed his ample stomach again. "The good side of it all, if you could consider it good, is that we would be treated better and we would not have to mourn a brother quite as often."

The strange applause similar to the whinnying of a horse was rendered with a lot of gusto.

Fuam jumped onto one of the stone tables for all to see her. She was dressed in a sleeveless coat made from the leather of some strange animal and open in the front to expose her chest and stomach.

The necklace on her throat was embedded with the tooth of a Mungongoh citizen that she had personally killed in battle during one of their early encounters. Her real age was difficult to guess, but it was believed that she had lived for more than ten generations of Mungongoh kings. Her strength and vigour were quite a contrast to the gnarled external features of her skin and scalp. Her shrivelled breasts looked like two used condoms dangling from her chest.

"Owners of Jvatein," she said loudly.

Jvatein was the original name of the planet when the dwarfs owned it alone before conquerors came in and renamed it Mungongoh, a name Fuam hated venomously and avoided mentioning completely. In all her speeches, she kept haranguing her people about the day that Jvatein will rise victorious like a phoenix from its ashes.

"Owners of Jvatein," she said. "You have heard Kanjam very well. I don't want to take decisions solo as we have a very democratic situation down here. Let's hear what all of you think. Should we allow ourselves to be hoodwinked by the occupants of our cherished planet?"

"We are going to be better off than before," said an old, bald dwarf. "Let us cooperate with the Ikwi."

"With Awobua gone and with this new monarch, who promises better things for the Mungongli, let us cooperate with the Ikwi," said another old dwarf.

"The people of Mungongoh have always been more powerful than us. There is virtually nothing we can do against them," said another dwarf. "So let's take advantage of the good things to come and work with them."

"Actually," said another bald-headed dwarf, "we have always been treated like underlings by the people of Mungongoh and we don't expect them to change overnight and treat us as equals. We should be satisfied with the improved status they seem ready to attribute to us."

"Finally," said one old female dwarf, "my children can work up there and bring back good food and good things to us without running the risk of being suddenly hammered to death."

"That is another thing, too," said a rotund dwarf. "The Ikwi people should have considered providing us with food and clothing."

"All of you are considering only the good things and forgetting that you shall be compelled to do their extractions for them," said Kanjam. "I learned the earthlings call it 'mining'."

Fuam was boiling with rage. She suddenly jumped up on the table, shouting and waving her hands in anger.

"All of this is hogwash! Baby talk! You are all chicken-hearted. I am really disappointed in you. You seem to have given up completely and are prepared to fully become Mungongoh slaves. Eeeh! How I hate that word, Mungongoh. Our planet here is called Jvatein, not that ridiculous name those creatures up there have given it."

Fuam glared round the room angrily, daring any dwarf to oppose her. Everybody remained respectfully silent.

"You cannot be talking about any harmonious coexistence with the enemy," she continued. "Have all of you forgotten that those creatures up there are the enemy? Don't be deceived by the fact that they are talking about better conditions for the Mungongli. Will they ever consider us as equals?"

Fuam looked around the horde of dwarfs to assess the impact of her fiery speech.

"What has gone wrong with the people of Jvatein? Our biggest wish has always been to drive away or eliminate by any means those intruders who now enjoy the fruits of our planet and have pushed us into holes, and this wish has not changed. We have remained in these caves for all this time because of the disunity between us. While we are looking for every way to make the lives of those fools up there uncomfortable, some of our brothers and sisters prefer to grovel at their feet and do all their menial jobs. On the other hand, they have always used a strong hand against us and have brutally crushed any of our attempts to take back what is ours."

The crowd was very attentive, and Fuam liked it. It was proof that her leadership position was still unchallenged.

"We have taken advantage of the fact that the lazy fellows use Mungongli for menial jobs and introduced a few spies like Kanjam right into the palace where all decisions are taken. Now, he has brought us good news, but what is good in the news is not the fact that the Mungongli shall be treated better and have a better status. The good news is that we now have a weak regime. We shall use this weakness to tactfully penetrate their guard and strike when they least expect. We shall take back our planet Jvatein."

There was awe in the atmosphere.

"She is right," said Kanjam. "From one of the Earth scenes that King Awobua watched, a certain Gorbachev, who was the president of the stiff Soviet Union, tried to soften things up and talked about perestroika or reconstruction. He introduced elements of democracy in an otherwise totalitarian state. A few smart guys took advantage of this and succeeded in throwing him out and taking over."

Kanjam looked at Fuam for approbation.

"With a change in their attitude towards Mungongli, they will not throw us to lions for the least transgressions. It will even take them time to figure out or realize that we are working at something, and it might be too late for them when we finally strike."

"Attacking them is still a big risk," said a careful dwarf. "They are still far stronger than us."

"That does not matter," said Fuam. "We shall plan and adopt a faultless strategy."

"Yes," Kanjam said. "The Mungongoh people intend to do a lot of trade with the earthlings but have discovered that they can only pay for the earthling's goods and services with what they call gold and precious stones. They will, thus, use us in what they call 'mines' to extract all these things for Mungongoh to use as payment."

"Can we not link up ourselves with these earthlings and supply them with these items?" asked one of the younger dwarfs. "After all, we have much of that down here, and we have better access to the items."

"We cannot do that officially. Mungongoh will not allow it," said Kanjam. "But, come to think a bit, we could do some smuggling."

"Some what?" Fuam asked.

"We could create some illegal and secret link with some of the earthlings who come in for the stuff, and supply them some of the items that we would pilfer from the mines."

"What shall we get from that?" Fuam asked.

"In the palace," said Kanjam, "we remain docile and stupid, but actually observe well. We don't miss any of the earth scenes that are watched there. From the various items that the earthlings make, there are several that they could smuggle into Mungongoh and supply to us, which could enable us to fight wars against Mungongoh. They have spears, bows and arrows, cutlasses, swords, guns, you name it. We have never succeeded in defeating Mungongoh in battle because we use our bare hands. We need an army that is trained and armed, and the earthlings can guarantee that for a reasonable quantity of those our pebbles."

"That is simply great," said Fuam. "We shall have to look into that."

Another dwarf jumped up.

"We know very little about earthlings and can't just go into any relationship with them," he said. "I once worked in the palace and, from the earth scenes, we understood that the

76

earth people were very cunning and double-crossing, especially the Americans. To settle in that country, which they now call theirs, the European invaders had to play a fast one on the indigenous Red Indians. They sold them guns so that they could easily kill each other and seriously reduce their populations, deceived them with strong alcoholic stuff, signed land conventions with them just to end up confiscating the land assigned to Indians, every dirty trick possible. Make an error with them and Mungongoh will go."

"How I hate that name," Fuam said behind clenched teeth. The name of this place is Jvatein, and usurpers have come in and given it a stupid name. Mungongoh, indeed. What difference does it make if the earthlings try to deceive us? At least they are far away, and we shall be very careful about the way we deal with them. How much worse can anything get from how these fools have made us animals in our own land?"

"I tell you the earthlings are worse than these present usurpers," replied the dwarf, who had worked in the palace. "They can sell anything for a profit, and would easily dispose of us if they were going to gain something. To deal with them, you have to be very smart and careful."

"Anyway," said another dwarf, "the people of Mungongoh will not let them get anywhere near us."

"Don't forget that a few of us work in the palace and are out there on your behalf," said Kanjam. "I can risk making contact with some of the earthlings."

"Well spoken," said Fuam. "We need patriots like you."

8

Following the series of meetings in the palace, Nyamfuka mobilized a team to carry out the first contact visits on Earth. The main task of this team was to establish contacts with the countries with which Mungongoh intended to develop diplomatic ties. All arrangements were made, and the team was ready to embark on its mission.

Nyamfuka and his team boarded a brand-new, magnificent space craft, specially constructed for important missions on Earth. They were not simply going out as agents on spying missions or as carriers of deadly diseases and products. They were now top officials on important diplomatic missions to Earth.

Funkuin had done everything to be a member of the delegation, using her position as the head of the AIDM and arguing that she must have first-hand knowledge of the Earth, which will be their main collaborators for now. Of course, there was a secondary motive in that she did not quite trust Nyamfuka alone with the sleek earthling girls.

Despite his advanced age, Professor Buh was also part of the team. His thorough knowledge of the history of the Earth, right from ancient times, was considered invaluable. There were two other members, a senior engineer and a professor in social sciences.

Despite the fact that Nyamfuka was the least educated among the elite diplomats, his considerable knowledge of Earth guaranteed his position as the head of the delegation.

As the craft took off and headed towards Earth, Nyamfuka sat down with his colleagues to discuss and plan their activities on Earth. They had taken along two dwarfs to serve them, and the little fellows bustled around serving drinks. Nyamfuka opted for a glass of abebe. He felt he needed the stiff drink, the closest thing to Earth's vodka, which he loved so much.

"Our flight will take five days," Nyamfuka told his colleagues, "but this craft has been decked out with every form of entertainment you can think of. We have arranged for the flight to be as comfortable as possible."

"It looks quite modern and comfortable," agreed Chiambah, the engineer who had been on a trip to Earth before.

"During the flight, we shall keep discussing our mission on Earth. We want to make the most out of it and go back to Mungongoh like heroes," Nyamfuka continued. "Luckily, we were carefully chosen and are all capable."

Nyamfuka gulped down his abebe, enjoyed the burning taste, and continued.

We are aware of all the countries we shall visit on Earth. If we start with America, they may want to influence our discussions with the other nations on our itinerary. I suggest we start with Nigeria and work our way up to end with America."

"I have a different opinion," said Funkuin. "We have worked with the Americans before in overthrowing King Awobua. They know about us and will easily be prepared to receive us. The other countries don't even know that we are coming, and their reception may be wanting. Let's go to America first, and then get the Americans to link us to the other nations."

"You may be right," said Nyamfuka, "but don't you think this will give the Americans the opportunity to influence our strategy and approach to setting up relations with the other countries?"

"Maybe," said Professor Buh, "but it would be better to start with the Americans we are sure of. Don't forget that diplomacy is something we have never practiced before. Let us start with America, although we should thread carefully."

"What do the others think?" asked Nyamfuka.

"Let us go to America first," said Mbeng.

"And you, Chiambah?" asked Nyamfuka.

"I support the idea of going to America first," said Chiambah.

"Okay," agreed Nyamfuka. "From America we go to Russia, Germany, and the rest."

In America, they no longer faced difficulties in meeting the President. The Americans were interested in the precious stones found in Mungongoh as well as the high tech. They had been struggling to perfect their flying saucer based on the blueprint that Fulumfuchong had left behind, but were still fogged about the most appropriate fuel to use. The Americans were also looking for opportunities for trade. They produced in abundance and needed thriving markets, such as Mungungoh, where food items were in short supply.

But the Americans were very hard and experienced negotiators. As predicted by Nyamfuka, they were pushing to control all relationships between Mungongoh and Earth. One negotiator was even talking about establishing what he called patent rights over Mungongoh. After all, he argued, it was America that discovered Mungongoh.

After one week of negotiations, the Mungongoh diplomats were quite exasperated. The good food and drink made available meant nothing again to Nyamfuka. He could have blown off some stress by sampling a few local girls, but this time he was stuck with Funkuin, and there was no possibility for any escapades.

Just as the team started wondering what to do next, they were contacted by a Russian spy. He made them understand that the Russians were more flexible and less greedy. He would arrange for them to cross over and meet the people of the Kremlin.

"Send a massage to them that we shall be in Russia as soon as possible," Nyamfuka told him.

"How are you traveling?" asked the spy. "Do you have a private jet?"

"Don't worry about that," said Nyamfuka. "Simply tell them to be expecting us."

When the spy left, Nyamfuka turned to his colleagues. "They have very crude crafts here that are called airplanes. We shall teleport ourselves to Russia and lay low for two days to give the impression that we moved across by one of their crude contraptions. Then we go to the Kremlin."

At the Kremlin the Prime Minister had just become the President and the President had become the Prime Minister. There was still some confusion as to who was playing what role when it came to the reception of the aliens. However, the Prime Minister seemed to be the man in control, and Nyamfuka concentrated on him.

"Why did you go to the Americans instead of coming to us?" the prime minister asked. "Those Americans can rip everything from your wonderful planet before you know of it. As for us Russians, we are interested in a fruitful relationship, a relationship that will make our nouveau rich richer, and we will introduce nice things to you like the ballet, vodka, and caviar."

"But can we trust you?" asked the President. "We don't want an aggressor from outer space."

That same evening, in the Hotel Rossia where the Mungongoh diplomats were lodged, they were approached by an American spy. The Americans had learnt of their disappearance and finally located them in Russia. It would be foolish to let go such a great friendship opportunity from which America had a lot to gain in the end. The soldiers who had participated in knocking off Awobua had come back with a picture of an Eldorado out there.

"America has decided to soften up," the spy said. "You can't trust the Russians. Better come back to the old friends you know."

"We will think about it," Nyamfuka said, dismissing the spy.

"The earthlings are a confused bunch of lunatics," observed Professor Buh once the spy had left.

"And very greedy, too," added Funkuin.

"So, chief, what do you think about the situation?" Chiambah asked Nyamfuka.

"I think I have gotten the reaction I wanted from the Americans," Nyamfuka said. "I suspected that when we came to Russia, the Americans would sober down. Anyway, we had planned to develop a link with Russia, too. We will go back to America and start from there as planned."

"You reasoned it out well, boss," said Mbeng. "When we get back to Russia, they will be only too ready to comply with our terms."

After going through all the countries they had planned and developing relationships, the team flew back satisfied to Mungongoh. The maiden diplomatic trip was over.

9

A meeting of AIDM was summoned to assess the success of the trip, but this time at the hall where meetings of the defunct IRDI used to take place. The structure had been renamed and the offices reallocated to current members. The meeting was now fully chaired by Funkuin, with Ngess attending as observer and adviser.

As the team leader, Nyamfuka presented a brief report to the eager audience.

"I hope you did not leave any children back there during your extended stay," Ndaba joked after Nyamfuka had finished presenting.

Funkuin frowned, "Ndaba, your big mouth will be clamped shut for you if you keep butting in with bawdy jokes when a respected member of the AIDM is talking."

"I hope you emphasized the fact that we don't want earthlings making their home here," said one of the old females.

"That is guaranteed," said Nyamfuka. "You see, only the Americans have a crude craft that can manage to get here, and we can easily destroy it if we don't want it to land. All the diplomats can only come and go using our crafts, and their stay here shall be very brief each time."

"That is wonderful," said Nange. "And what of our own diplomatic missions on Earth?"

"We agreed with the earthlings that since they will be allowed to have only visiting diplomats out here in Mungongoh, we shall also limit our missions to visiting diplomats."

"For how long will they be allowed to stay when they come?" asked the female with the screechy voice.

"We proposed a maximum of one week to them," said Chiambah.

"One week is too long already," said the stern looking dame.

"True," said Yivissi. "Earthlings can do terrible things within a week."

"Okay," said Funkuin, "let us limit it to two days each time."

"I am more comfortable with that," said Professor Buh.

"But then," said Nange, "where do they stay when they are here? Do we put them up in our homes?"

"On Earth," said Nyamfuka, "they have hotels. We shall have to construct one in a hurry."

"It should be constructed close to the palace," said Funkuin, "where we can always keep an eye on them. They should be closely watched and controlled. Some palace guards should be specially trained to keep them in check when they are here."

"But they are diplomats," protested Nyamfuka. "They are supposed to have diplomatic immunity and should be treated with a lot of respect."

"We don't care much about that," said Funkuin. "If they want to come to Mungongoh, they must come on our terms."

"I support what Professor Funkuin has said," said the screechy voice. "We are already making a huge sacrifice by accepting them. I have two grown-up daughters, and I don't want them anywhere near an earthling."

"Are there going to be females among these diplomats?" asked a handsome middle aged woman. "I would like to have an earthling female as a friend."

"And have her flirting with your husband the next minute?" asked Funkuin. "Earthling women are known to be

86

very untrustworthy. Give them the slightest chance, and you end up sharing your man with them."

"Not all of them are like that," said Nyamfuka. "I have come across tough, upright females on earth."

"That does not cancel out the fact that many of them are sluts," said Funkuin. "And we don't know which ones will come here as diplomats. Let us declare that we will not accept female diplomats."

"Hey!" said Nyamfuka. "Who is more vulnerable? Our girls and wives or our husbands?"

There was general laughter.

"Instead," continued Nyamfuka, "I suggest that the earthling diplomats come with their wives or earthling females. That way, the female earthlings will distract the horny males from so much as ogling our females. Female earthlings are quite jealous, I can tell you."

"However, until we are comfortable with them, we won't allow them to stay that long," said Ngess. "We shall start by taking them back the same day, as soon as they are through with whatever they came to do."

"I am still totally against the idea of considering developing relationships with humans," said the hawkish female member of the AIDM. "Humans have very revolting habits that can rub off on us and our offspring. We should eat with them with very long spoons if we must hobnob with them, but I think we should have nothing to do with them completely. The American soldiers have left, and that should be the end of it all."

"What of their children, who will soon be born?" asked Nyamfuka. "A few of them strayed with our girls and the results are there."

"We shall find a way to handle that," said the hawkish female. "Actually, I am already working on that in my laboratory."

"But some of the Americans looked so gentle and nice. Why do some of you distrust them so much?" asked Fulumfuchong.

"I was once a Mungongoh agent on earth," said the professor with the walrus moustache, "and we have learnt to disapprove of many things that happen on Earth. They only go for profit and hardly ever consider sacrificing for anything."

"I can quite understand him," said Nyamfuka. "Most Mungongoh agents resent the wasteful habits of the earthlings when we have little in Mungongoh."

"Not only in Mungongoh," said the old professor. "Even in many parts of Earth children die by the thousands from starvation while trash cans in other areas are full of good food, jettisoned by blokes who have too much."

"I, too, noticed that while on Earth," said another former agent. "You see tasty cheese, sausages, and fruits thrown away by the people who could afford to buy too much but could not muster the appetite to eat it; meanwhile, those with the appetite are starving."

"You even see rotten flesh left in some of the bushes because an animal was killed just for its skin or tusks, and the carcass was abandoned to rot."

"That is it," said the old professor. "While on Earth, I came across a book by this chap called Voltaire. In the book, titled 'Candide', he reasons that when cannibals kill, it is not a crime; they are simply looking for food. It is the same as humans killing bison or deer for their meat. On the other hand, when you kill other human beings and do not consume them, but rather abandon them to rot, then you have committed a grievous crime. Cannibals kill only what they want to eat, but criminals raze down hundreds of valiant youths in their prime for no other reason than to win one useless battle or another or to defend some unclear cause. Look at the crusades."

"The wastefulness on Earth is highest," said Ngess, "when it comes to what they term the lucky class. For running around a field and kicking a football, for playing tennis or golf or simply for shrieking and prancing up and down on stage, they earn fabulously. They attribute these absurdly inflated incomes to talent."

"How could this class waste more than wars?" asked the old professor. "Imagine how many persons were killed during the Second World War alone."

"That," replied Ngess, "is a form of waste that occurs through violence. What I am talking about is a form of waste that is apparently not prominent but quite serious. One of the Earth's classic authors, Thorstein Veblen, refers to them simply as the leisure class and describes them as conspicuous consumers of goods. While consuming publicly and conspicuously, they produce nothing useful but strive to show that they can consume more than other members of their class."

"That is the best description for those fatheads who call themselves celebrities and upper class," said Ndaba.

"That is my boy," replied Ngess. "You see, in their bloated view of less fortunate humans, they often dismiss them as lazy bums, not prepared to work hard."

"Some of them, however, give assistance to the less fortunate," said Nyamfuka.

"Yes, but what percentage of their wealth is given to charity? Most of them prefer to compete to be the richest person on earth. Others want to see their latest gold watch, villa, or expensive cars publicized in all the papers and news media."

"Anyway," said the king, "there is nothing we can do about the gross inequality on Earth. We simply have to know how to collaborate with them and come out unscathed."

The king took a sip from the drink the dwarfs had served him. There was no longer a special drink for the king alone.

10

The first diplomats from America that were received in Mungongoh were ten in number, well-dressed in dark suits. They had arrived in a cream coloured space craft that the king had sent to Earth to transport them to Mungongoh. They were received at the earth port by Nyamfuka, who led them to the king. At the earth port, there was no elaborate reception ceremony, and the Americans were simply transported in swift floating vehicles to the palace. As they moved into the king's presence, they bowed gracefully and waited to be ushered to their seats. Nyamfuka took care of this aspect, and very soon they were seated.

The earthlings looked around, awed by the splendour and simplicity of the room in which they were seated. Some of the Americans who were acquainted with or had seen pictures of traditional dresses in Kom and parts of the North West Region of Cameroon realized that the Mungongoh people dressed very similarly, only the Mungongoh dresses were finer and flawless.

The king was resplendent in a beautifully-made dalla, and his presence was further brightened by the radiant queen Yivissi, who was dressed in a matching female-cut dalla. The throne was simple, but the abundant precious material embedded in the raised pedestal, the seats of the king and queen, and the walls around the throne made the Americans' eyes glimmer with lust. On the other side of the hall, the members of the AIDM were all seated, dressed in their best.

"You are welcome to Mungongoh," the king said. "We hope you had a nice trip. Thank you for agreeing to start up a friendly relationship with us. We hope to develop a faithful co-existence with you that will be beneficial to the people of America and the people of Mungongoh."

"Thank you, Sir, ehm, Your Majesty," said the head of the American delegation, Mr. Dubson. "We are happy that you accepted to receive us and even sent a space craft to bring us here."

"You are welcome," said the king, "although we were not expecting so many of you." The king looked around the room. "Yes, there are too many of you on this mission. Do you need ten persons to come here to discuss this relationship of ours?"

The king's tone was not harsh but firm. He calmed down as the queen stretched out a hand and touched him lightly on the arm.

"Who have you come with?" he asked the American.

"I am sorry, sir, about the size of our delegation; however, by our standards, this is a small delegation, sir," said Dubson. "We came along with experts in different fields since we thought you were fully prepared to work with us."

"We are," said Ngess, "but we don't want things to move too fast. We still have to take our time and learn to trust you. We are still wary about this relationship, and with good reason, too. You see, for all these years we have been observing the Earth very closely; and, from the things we've seen happening, we find it difficult to completely trust any country out there."

"We quite understand your trepidation," said Mr. Dubson, "but you see, for us to collaborate, you must trust us somehow. You trusted us when it came to overthrowing your former king, remember?"

"That was because we were desperate," said the king. "Besides, Awobua's demise was in the interest of both of us.

His lust for the Earth was immeasurable, and the Earth, including America, was really in peril."

"You see, your highness," said the American, "diplomatic representation is a delicate thing. We need experts in all the fields so as not to make mistakes. As I was saying, this is a rather small delegation if we are to discuss things at length or establish a concrete relationship. Here we have Professor Robin, head of NASA space program, Mr. Hummingbird, the editor-in-chief of Newsweek magazine, Reverend Grub of the Ebenezer Baptist Church, and Mr. Zibanchuk, a business man and Wall Street magnet. Next, Professor Fiddle of the Michigan State University and Dr. Butelbroad, Psychiatrist and Philosopher. The lady there is Miss Mayfair, special adviser in the Whitehouse. Next to her is Mrs. O'buttocks, senior diplomat and negotiator. Finally, you have General Steak of the U.S. Army and my humble self, Mr. Dubson, of the State Department."

"Although you did not have to come along with so many people during your first trip," Funkuin said, "I am happy that you came along with some women."

"As you see, Madame, this group is very representative of America. We need to work in as many fields as possible."

"This thickest man you call "steak" or whatever," said Funkuin, "is, from what I understand, a soldier. What is a soldier doing here? We don't want war."

"We could eventually form military alliances, Madame, or sell you some of our weapons," replied General Steak calmly.

"We don't want weapons and we don't want wars," the queen said. "Next time, don't bring this "steak" along when you are coming to Mungongoh."

This time she was talking to the leader of the American delegation.

"This is your first trip, and you are already hiding something from us," said Ngess. "This "steak" you call General brought along many armed soldiers. You never mentioned that there were soldiers in your delegation."

Nyamfuka stood up and moved over to the American delegation.

"May I apologize on their behalf," he said to the Americans. "Here in Mungongoh we are very straightforward. We have never before taken the time to acquire appropriate diplomatic language. I am aware that on Earth diplomats use pretentious and flowery language when engaged in formal discussions."

"We understand that," said Dubson. "Besides, being gentlemen, we have learned to tolerate patiently the unpredictable female attitude."

"Now, may I ask why you came along with a General of the Army and so many soldiers?" Nyamfuka said. "It was not difficult for us to discover that."

"We are sorry about that," said Mr. Dubson. "The General's presence here is no threat. His mission is clean. As for the soldiers, we took them along because of uncertainties. You can see that they have stayed in the craft and have not set foot on Mungongoh. They shall remain there till we take off. We hope that on subsequent visits you will allow us to bring them along."

The meeting continued for five hours with the Americans trying to be as diplomatic as ever and the members of AIDM trying to be as cautious as ever. When the meeting finally came to an end, the Americans were surprised that, instead of giving them a welcome party or even dinner and then showing them to their hotel rooms, they were led from the palace straight to the earth port where their spacecraft was waiting to take them back to earth. Mungongoh was taking no chances.

During the meeting, the members of the AIDM had left virtually no room for haggling. They had stated their points clearly. They were interested in trade, especially for food items, and would pay in precious stones. A conversion rate would be worked out according to the item concerned. They were also interested in sports and games and certain forms of entertainment. But they wanted nothing to do with the military. The American diplomats sent to Mungongoh would not be permitted to live permanently there, but would remain in America, paying only brief, periodic visits or coming if an emergency came up.

The Americans were not quite satisfied as they boarded the flying saucer and took off for America. They had not been permitted to see as much of Mungongoh as they would have wanted. They resented the way they had been ferried from the earth port to the palace in sealed floating vehicles and brought back to the earth port immediately after. However, what they had seen in the palace would make anyone's mouth water. All the vases, jars, and other vessels were of pure gold or silver or some exquisitely beautiful material. The floors were marble. The tables were of a very rich alloy, and the ceiling was of a rich material studded with emeralds. All materials used were expertly polished and very attractive.

The earthlings had also noticed the dwarfs, who sat on low stools in the corner and rushed to serve whenever there was a request for their services.

The dwarfs had stunted legs, and their heads had a flat surface at the top. The dwarfs were certainly reserved for menial duties in Mungongoh, but they seemed contented and ready to oblige.

"Those guys up there are nuts," said General Steak. "How can a nation exist without an army? That is quite absurd, and they have so much to protect and defend."

"They are a confused bunch of beings," concurred Zibanchuk, the Wall Street magnate. "Imagine how much money we could have made in arms sales."

"You want to supply them with arms that they can use tomorrow against us?" asked Miss Mayfair.

"They look very simple," said the head of the delegation, "but they are certainly more sophisticated in technology. Look at their crafts."

"Their level of technology is certainly quite high, Mr. Dubson," said Mrs. O'Buttocks. "I am sure they could make far more sophisticated weapons."

"I was very vigilant," said General Steak. "Those palace guards are equipped only with things that looked like truncheons. I am convinced that there are no fire arms on this planet."

"You saw how strongly they rejected anything to do with the military," said Professor Robin. "I wish the earth could be like that."

"You admire those crazy fellows for doing nothing about their defence?" asked General Steak.

"That is just what is wrong with the earth," said Professor Robin. Under the umbrella of defence, countries spend a fortune on arms to the detriment of development. I tell you, the world would be a far better place if we stopped talking about Defence and spending lavishly on it, whereas half the world is living under stress and lack food and basic comfort."

"The people of Mungongoh are on the right path," said Mrs. O'Buttocks.

"But I tell you, the people are rich," exclaimed Zibanchuk. "Our moguls, Croesus, and the oil sheiks put together can come nowhere near that King Fulumfuchong. Could you assess the wealth in that palace?"

"Let us remain level-headed," advised Reverend Grub. "We should tread carefully and build up a concrete and lasting relationship with the people of Mungongoh. We could easily convert all of them to Christianity, and then we could peacefully exploit all the resources of Mungongoh before they see it coming."

"What of Russia and the other countries that were invited?" asked Miss Mayfair.

"We are working on the Mungongoh people with tact," said Mr. Dubson. "We shall convince them that, for now, they don't need any other partner on earth."

"Is that so?" asked Zibanchuk.

"Yes," replied the head of the delegation. "You noticed that the people out there in Mungongoh are panicky about the possibility of many people from Earth coming to their planet. For now, only America has the blueprint of one of these space craft, and Mungongoh knows that. They know that for nothing in the world would America give out this blueprint, that this valuable technology is well-protected. For now, only Munongoh can send flying saucers to transport people from these other nations to Mungongoh. I am sure that, at least for quite a while, they will not want to transport smart Russians and Germans here for fear that their technology might be copied and their spacecrafts mass produced and made available to any adventurer who can afford to buy one."

"That makes me think of something, General Steak," said Miss Mayfair.

"And what would that be?" asked the General.

"The dwarfs in the palace," she replied. "They were playing a menial role."

"And how does that interest you?" asked General Steak.

"If they are subjected to menial jobs, then there must be some degree of disgruntlement in them."

"Yes?" the general asked.

"There should be a great many dwarfs on that planet. We could exploit their disgruntlement and provide them with arms to revolt."

"And what do we gain from that?" asked Mrs O' Buttocks.

"Can't you see?" said Miss Mayfair. "With the dwarfs armed and revolting, Mungongoh will have to buy arms from us. That will be a big deal."

"You have a point there," said General Steak. "And there is still something else that we can gain from arming the dwarfs."

"Let's hear it," said Mr. Dubson.

"If we were to support the dwarfs to fight and take over, it might be more profitable to do business with the less intelligent and less suspicious dwarfs."

"Just hear yourselves talk," said Mrs. O'Buttocks. "You have not yet entered Mungongoh and you are already thinking of setting the whole place on fire. If you create chaos there, how do you suppose to do business with them?"

"With chaos in the place," said General Steak, "we can easily crush both dwarfs and Mungongoh citizens and take over the place."

"Wonderful, we will have all that Eldorado to ourselves," Zibanchuk said.

Actually, Zibanchuk had a different idea. He had listened keenly to the conversation that had just transpired and gathered much to transmit to his masters. Out in Mungongoh, he had been attentive, but the extra caution adopted against the earthlings by their Mungongoh hosts prevented him from gathering much information for his masters. While in the palace, he had noted that Mungongoh was certainly a rich place. He had also noted the existence of dwarfs playing the role of servants. But this conversation by the members of the team had opened his eyes further. He now had solid information for his masters. At least his trip could be considered a resounding success.

Back on earth, the members of the Mungongoh delegation were summoned to a top secret meeting with the president of America.

"Welcome from your trip into the cosmos," the president said smiling. "I hope you had a good time out there and did much for America."

The President was unaware of the fact that there was an infiltrator right inside the team of well-vetted personalities.

"The people of Mungongoh were not quite friendly, sir," replied the head of the delegation. "They took us from the earth port, as they call it, to the palace and after the meeting, they took us right back to the earth port. The usual American hospitality was completely absent."

"We have to cope with that," said President Mboma. "They certainly have their own ways, which we must respect."

"Strange ways if you ask me," said General Steak. "The people are too stiff and arrogant; however, there are disgruntled dwarfs out there that we could use to foment trouble. Then we would have the opportunity to move in and impose our ways on those recluses. Would you imagine, sir, that they are not interested in arms and defence?"

"We need to act according to what the General has proposed, sir," said Miss Mayfair. "We don't want any complications in our relationship with Mungongoh. Much is at stake out there, and Mungongoh has the intention of dealing with all nations on earth. This could give the Russians the possibility of grabbing a considerable part. On the other hand, dealing with the dwarfs directly could change things and enable us to have our way."

'God,' thought the Christian President, 'I made the error of sending real hawks out there.'

"Don't say that again," President Mboma said, sternly. "We are going to Mungongoh to make friends not war."

"But you need to see how much wealth there is, sir," said one of the team members. "That throne alone is worth a fortune."

"May I remind you," said the President, who was quite disappointed with the team, "that what you are saying is very remote from the purpose of our mission in Mungongoh."

"Mr. Dawson," President Mboma continued, "I want a more reasonable team on these trips to Mungongoh, not persons of a rapacious disposition."

"I will see to that, sir," Dawson said.

11

From the reception in the White House, the space travellers were taken to a hotel where rooms had been reserved for them. As the others settled in their rooms, Zibanchuk slipped out of his, went out of the hotel, and hailed a taxi. The taxi took him to a location on the outskirts of Washington where he got out and waited for the taxi to depart. After looking around furtively, he moved up to a small brick house and knocked gently in a kind of code. The door was flung open by a hooded person, and he slipped inside.

"I need to communicate urgently with the High One," he said to the other occupant of the brick house.

"You won't go to Atlantis?" the hooded person asked.

"The message is quite urgent, and I don't think I have enough time," Zibanchuk answered.

"I would advise you to make time and go right to Atlantis," the hooded person said. "You are aware of the modern technology available to the FBI and the CIA to trace secret messages, and I suppose you are equally aware of the severe punishment that the High One metes out for carelessness."

"I think you are right," Zibanchuk said. "Convey me to Atlantis."

Down in the deepest part of the Atlantic Ocean within the Bermuda triangle was the underground headquarters of the most secret and most powerful criminal organization on earth - Musoh. The inner core of this organization had one hundred members who lived in this underwater abode called Atlantis. The head of this organization was simply known as the High One, and from Atlantis he and his innermost core controlled the whole organization. It was difficult to determine his sex, but easy to discern the cruelty that lay beneath the bland face. The High One was unforgiving and cruel, and there was no restraint in him when he suspected the slightest carelessness or weakness in any of his subordinates. Part of this cold and inflexible attitude towards other fellow humans might have been due to the fact that the High One was either totally not interested in sex or not capable of having sex. It was suspected by the members of the club of one hundred that he neither had the male nor the female sex organs.

To the club of one hundred, every comfort imagined on earth was available. However, no sex was allowed in Atlantis, a law understandably imposed by the High One. The members of the club of one hundred were thus deprived of this most coveted pleasure on earth for a good part of the year. They could only indulge in sex during their vacations, which permitted them to come out of Atlantis and enjoy the pleasures of the earth. Each member had three one month long vacations each year, and they took turns. That way, there were always enough members of the inner core with whom the High One could discuss and take key decisions when necessary.

Another group of one thousand members were at the second level and operated all over the world, following instructions from Atlantis. Among these were doctors, lawyers, and other professionals at very high levels, as well as businessmen. They occupied high positions in whichever country and in whatever organization they operated. Members of the club of one thousand had access to great affluence in the countries where they were operating. They visited Atlantis three times a year. During these one week long visits, they gave full reports on their activities and got further instructions.

Belonging to the Musoh organization at the two highest levels could be quite lucrative, but a lot of sacrifice went along with it. The organization employed about one million persons most of whom were completely ignorant about their real employer.

All top priority missions were reported directly to the High One. Mungongoh was a top priority mission, and Zibanchuk had been specially fitted into the team on diplomatic mission to Mungongoh. To succeed in fitting people into places, Musoh used influence, money, and threats.

Using the special secret passage, Zibanchuk arrived in Atlantis and was received by the High One. He gave a very vivid description of everything that had transpired in Mungongoh and, using ideas from the team's conversations on their way back to earth, presented a satisfying analysis of the situation. At the end, he was happy to receive congratulations from the High One, though in an icy tone. It was rare for the High One to congratulate anyone. Based on Zibanchuk's report, the High One summoned a meeting of the club of one hundred.

The meeting was held in a lavish sitting accommodation that could beat all the top class fittings in the first class section of the Titanic. The absence of sexual satisfaction in Atlantis was compensated for with all the luxury and comfort imaginable. The seats in the meeting hall were of the best material and every other facility was of the best quality.

The services were impeccable. The best quality champagne, whiskeys, and brandies were available in abundance alongside caviar, lobsters, crab, and other delicacies. There was food from all over the world for each member to indulge according to his or her taste. Food and drink were always available for all to sample, giving room for overindulging. However, there were two items that always went with the food and drink to counter the effects of overindulging. One was a capsule that prevented you from getting drunk and totally eliminated any possibilities of a hangover or other after effects of alcohol. The other was a pinkish liquid that kept your stomach quite fine and enabled you to muck down as much food as your appetite permitted without any uncomfortable consequences.

Apart from meetings, the members of the club of one hundred often gathered in this large room to socialize with one another when they were not engaged in individual pursuits such as swimming, sleeping, watching entertaining programs, or engaged in some enjoyable distractions - apart from sex of course. Generally, the members of this club spent most of their time involved in one form of leisure or another. The only thing they engaged in that could be described as work was when they gathered in this room for meetings to make key discussions.

12

It was time for the next diplomatic mission to Mungongoh. President Mboma made sure that all the hawkish elements in the team were struck off. Mr. Dubson still remained at the head of the team. Reverend Grub stayed on, and it was agreed that General Steak should be replaced by a representative of the C.I.A. The President was unaware of the fact that this last decision had been influenced by a powerful organization.

Back in the C.I.A, it took some convincing, backed by other forces, to get Mr. Hawk fitted into the team as the representative of the C.I.A. The next trip to Mungongoh thus had an official team endorsed by the President and was expected to bring back better results.

After an uneventful journey, they finally landed in Mungongoh. Their reception in Mungongoh was the same as before. They were taken straight from the earth port to the palace where they sat down for discussions. It was astonishing how the people of Mungongoh could switch over and speak English so easily.

The C.I.A operative, James Hawk, was wondering whether the dwarfs had the capacity of speaking and understanding the English language. He was watching them closely as they sat in their corner, attentive to any possible demand for one service or another by the Mungongoh citizens and their guests. He noticed with interest that the Mungongoh negotiators spoke to the dwarfs in the same strange language. The dwarfs for their part never spoke to each other through out, and it was not possible to make out whether they had another language of their own.

The C.I.A fellow's concentration on the dwarfs was interrupted by an announcement that whoever needed a toilet should beckon one of the dwarfs to take him there. He had been trying to figure out how best to contact one of the dwarfs, and here was the chance handed to him on a platter of gold. The only problem now would be whether it would be possible to communicate with a dwarf in English.

After a short while Hawk took his chance and indicated to one of the dwarfs that he needed his attention. His trained eye had enabled him to choose a dwarf that was most likely to cooperate. The fellow came across and stood waiting.

"Take me to the toilet, please," Hawk said in a loud tone for all to hear.

To his satisfaction, the dwarf replied in perfect English. "This way, sir," the dwarf said, leading.

In the corridor outside the hall, Hawk asked whether he could read.

"All dwarfs in this palace can read, sir," the dwarf replied. "We can speak, read, and write the Mungongoh language and all the languages on Earth that are written.

"Good," said Hawk, removing a piece of paper from his pocket and handing it over to the dwarf.

"How many dwarfs are there in Mungongoh?" Hawk asked.

"I couldn't say, sir," said the dwarf, "but there are many more of us than Mungongoh citizens."

"Good," said Hawk again. "Enjoin your colleagues to read what I have handed over to you. We think we can help you take over and rule Mungongoh. Wouldn't you want that?"

"I will discuss it with my people, sir," the dwarf replied. "The toilets are this way, sir."

"Wait a minute," Hawk said. "How do I get your reply?"

"Make sure you are on the next trip to Mungongoh," the dwarf replied. "I shall contact you then. Now hurry before the people in there get suspicious."

After the meeting, the Americans were bundled back to the earth port for their return trip. Hawk was silent as the others were excitedly recounting the success they had had during the meeting. Deep inside his heart, Hawk knew that he had achieved much more than the others put together.

13

Two days later, the dwarfs were gathered in their usual Ayissi for another important meeting. They had been summoned by Fuam, who claimed she had valuable information to share. She was standing by the table on which she usually stood to talk to her people. By her side were two neat dwarfs, an indication that they worked in the palace or some big institution.

"We have very good news," Fuam announced as she climbed on the table and dragged one of the dwarfs up with her. This time it was not Kanjam but a dwarf called Tubuo. Kanjam was the other neat dwarf present, and he stood smiling from ear to ear.

"Fellow Mungongli," Fuam said. "It is time we threw off the shackles of serfdom and reclaimed what is ours. Jvatein shall be free from usurpers."

There was heavy applause from the floor while Fuam beamed like a satisfied child.

"I shall hand over to Tubuo to give you the good news. Listen to him carefully and judge for yourselves."

"Fellow Mungongli," Tubuo said at the top of his raucous voice. "Listen to me carefully. We may be about to make a break-through. When the Mungongoh usurpers decided to establish a relationship with the earthlings and allow them to visit our planet now and again, they did not know that they were looking for trouble for themselves."

There was hushed silence as everybody listened attentively.

"Yesterday earthlings came and were received at the royal palace. Despite close supervision and care, one of them managed to slip across a letter asking the Mungongli to connive with them and clear off the Mungongoh Ikwi from this planet."

The reaction from the floor was confused. While some faces registered shock, other Mungungli were shouting with joy. "They are expecting our reply during their next visit here."

"Wait a minute," said a plump dwarf. "The earthlings have not even developed a relationship fully with Mungongoh and they are already planning to knock them off? These are not the kind of persons we should do business with. We can't trust them. How can we be sure that they will not turn around tomorrow and treat us the same way?"

"That is a good point you have raised," said Kanjam. "We need to be careful with the earthlings. We are already aware of that. For now, our enemy is the Ikwi. If, with the help of the earthlings, we could dispose of them, let us seize the chance. Afterwards we shall know how to protect ourselves against the earthlings."

"The aspect of overthrowing the Mungongoh usurpers and taking over what belongs to us is too tempting. We should not give up such an opportunity just because of a little distrust for the earthlings," said Fuam.

"We have to be careful though," said Tubuo.

'Sure,' said Fuam. 'We have to be careful. Of course.

14

During the next trip to Mungongoh, Hawk beckoned the same dwarf to lead him to the toilet. Out in the corridor, the dwarf had a reply to his previous request.

"The Mungongli are prepared to cooperate with you Americans," he whispered.

"Who are the Mungongli?" Hawk whispered back.

"The dwarfs, I mean," replied Tubuo. "We call ourselves Mungongli, and there is nothing we want more badly than to remove the Mungongoh usurpers from our planet."

"You could even make them slaves, too," Hawk said, "and compel them to serve you the way you serve them."

"We don't have much time, Tubuo said. "How do you suppose we work this out?"

"Mobilize yourselves into an organized army," Hawk said. "That is what you should do. Apart from the palace guards, Mungongoh has no army. They simply lord it over you because you guys are afraid to confront them. On the day of the uprising, we shall come in with some American marines, the type of soldiers who were brought in to overthrow Awobua. These soldiers are used to brute force. For your part, cut out rocks that you can use as clubs, or mould clubs from clay."

"How do we determine the day of the uprising?" Tubuo asked.

"You regularly serve in the palace where all decisions are taken. Hint to your fellow dwarfs that all of you should keep your ears open. When the king announces the day for our next visit, that will be the day."

"How do we trust you?" Tubuo asked.

"America is the most reliable ally you can have," Hawk said. "You should have every trust in us."

"But you are just trying to betray the Mungongoh people who have declared friendship and want to collaborate with you," Tubuo said.

"It is not the same thing," Hawk said. "We are doing this because we realize that you dwarfs are poorly treated out here. You know that we helped Mungongoh to overthrow Awobua because of the harsh tyranny of his reign. America always wants fairness and always steps in to support those who are being trampled upon or poorly treated. You dwarfs should actually be represented in that elite team that meets with us at the palace."

The naïf Tubuo was convinced.

15

The next night, the dwarfs gathered for another meeting. This time, there were five dwarfs from the palace.

"There is much progress, my people," Fuam announced, as she jumped on the table. "It is now certain that we shall have the support to beat the Ikwi. Tubuo made contact with the earthlings and will speak directly to you."

"Tubuo climbed up and met her on the table.

"Fellow Mungongli," he said. "It is all fixed. For the next trip, the earthlings are coming here with soldiers to help us fight. These are very well trained soldiers of the calibre that came here to overthrow King Awobua. Our weakness against the Ikwi is that we have never been organized. The earthling advises that we should have an army and carve out heavy stones that we could use as clubs to pound the Ikwi to death."

The reaction of the dwarfs was spontaneous. The whinnying sound filled the whole Ayissi and all around, a sign that the dwarfs were contented with the situation that had been developed.

There were still a few of them who shouted out, expressing worry.

"What if the Americans turn on us after defeating the Ikwi?" one of them asked.

"Rest assured that they won't," Tubuo said. "The earthlings are coming as our allies."

"I would not trust the earthlings to respect such a loose agreement," said the careful dwarf. "After all, they are already plotting against the Ikwi with whom they have just developed friendship ties."

"They assured me," said Tubuo, "that their problem with the Ikwi is that they are treating the Mungongli unfairly and the earthlings want fairness."

The whinnying sound rose again in a round of applause. The careful dwarfs were overwhelmed.

16

During the meeting called by the High One of the Musoh organization after receiving Zibanchuk's report, it had been resolved that everything should be done to make Mungongoh a personal property of the Musoh organization. This decision had been put into action immediately, and Hawk was identified as the key operative. Hawk was one of the members of the club of one thousand who had been fitted into the C.I.A. Through their usual means, the Musoh had succeeded in making Hawk a member of the second diplomatic team to Mungongoh.

The Musoh never did things in half measures. They were fully aware of the fact that taking over Mungongoh meant that they had to have a thorough knowledge of the place. Further, they had to construct their own space craft. Their next move, therefore, was to trace one of the soldiers who had participated in the deposing of Awobua and lure him into disclosing information about all that he had seen in Mungongoh. They were quite happy and satisfied with the information that there were no fire arms, rockets, or modern sophisticated defensive systems in Mungongoh. They could, therefore, concentrate on the construction of their own flying saucers.

Through their secret links, they knew that the Americans had constructed a prototype of the Mungongoh flying saucer based on blueprints left behind by a Mungongoh engineer. In their underground world, they had better scientists, held captive, and super high-tech equipment. They had already produced a craft that the High One used whenever he wanted to come up to the world outside. The craft moved at a speed faster than light when it left the water and could not be detected by radar. He could thus move to whatever part of the world he desired unnoticed. All they needed now was to get a copy of the blueprints for the Mungongoh flying saucer. It was not easy and cost the Musoh a fortune to get. With the plan available, they had embarked on construction of two crafts. Their underwater construction sites could not be penetrated by Mungongoh high-tech observation systems, so construction went on undetected by Mungongoh.

Two hundred mercenaries had been tactically selected and were being trained for the mission to Mungongoh. During his previous trip to Mungongoh, Hawk had been very observant and had noticed that Mungongoh did not seem to be prepared for attacks from foreign assailants. The earth port was unguarded and, from the earth port to the palace, he had not noticed any soldiers or police apart from the poorly armed palace guards. From thorough analysis of the preparations that took place before American marines were dispatched to Mungongoh, he had discovered that the Mungongoh people could not be killed by mere gunfire. They could be clubbed into submission or death with the use of heavy objects. They could equally be torn to pieces, but their wounds healed fast so the tearing had to be fast and massive.

As for the dwarfs, they were more populous than the citizens of Mungongoh, from what the dwarfs had said. With them out of their dungeons and swarming all over the place to distract the Mungongoh citizens, the Musoh mercenaries would easily get a foothold and enable the dwarfs to take over. It would be easier to out-manoeuvre the dwarfs eventually.

The Musoh had already analysed the profitability of ownership of Mungongoh. Apart from the wealth that lay within the crust of the small planet, there was a lot to be gained from tourism. Americans and other rich Europeans would pay a fortune to visit a place like that for a few days. He was already dreaming of world-class hotels and other tourist facilities.

Hawk was a much-respected senior official of the C.I.A and had access to the top most secrets. He could easily push himself into any task he wanted and had the full confidence of his bosses.

Attending the last meeting in the White House, during which the date of departure for the next visit and the date of arrival in Mungongoh was set, Hawk was very attentive. During the meeting the President insisted on peace, caution, and respect for Mungongoh.

Immediately after the meeting, and armed with invaluable information, Hawk went to a hotel room he had booked, quite satisfied. That night, he pulled out a harmless looking watch from under his undergarments in his suitcase and replaced the watch on his arm with it. It looked quite ordinary, but was actually a very powerful transmitter. He went out of the hotel, took a taxi to another part of town, and entered one of those night bars. Inside the bar, he took a stiff drink and then moved to a toilet where he locked the door carefully and switched on the watch.

"Chameleon to Green Mamba, Chameleon to Green Mamba!"

"Green Mamba listening, over," a voice crackled from the other end.

Green Mamba was the contact Hawk had in Atlantis and a member of the club of one hundred. It had been determined that certain circumstances could prevent Hawk from getting right to Atlantis to report to the High One so this contact was created. It was forbidden to communicate with the High One directly through communication systems.

"This is very urgent," Hawk whispered into the transmitter. "Are you through with the construction of the ovens?" Hawk asked.

"Almost."

Oven was their secret name for flying saucers.

"And the training of our cooks?"

"Almost complete," the voice crackled again over the line.

Cook was the secret name for mercenaries.

"You better hurry," Hawk said. "Things shall start on the seventh day from now at twelve midnight. Don't forget the time difference. Time span is five days, so I expect you to be fully on time and fully prepared. We may not communicate again unless there are changes."

Hawk switched off, flushed the toilet, and slipped out to the street for a drink at another bar before he took a taxi to his hotel.

17

The dwarfs had set to work. They had found an underground clay deposit and were now moulding clay into clubs. They had no appropriate instruments for hewing out clubs from rock so they had opted for clay. As some of the dwarfs expertly moulded the clubs from clay, others contrived to use heat from the rock that served as a source of fuel for Mungongoh flying saucers to harden them.

With the set of clubs ready, Fuam rallied the dwarf leaders and declared that it was time for training to start.

Training was quite a clumsy process. There was no qualified instructor experienced in warfare or organized battle. They had been engaged in pitched battles before with the invading Mungongoh, but these were always spontaneous and involved individual initiative. Military strategy was not known, and leadership in battle was a loose concept to them. Fuam had emerged as a leader because she was responsible for most Mungongoh dead and was always the last to scamper off in front of threatening Mungongoh fighters.

Mungongoh, too, had neither trained soldiers nor a standing army. The king's guards had led in battle against the untrained and disorganized dwarf hordes, and so the dwarfs had never had the chance of learning anything from the enemy. They had seen Mungongoh palace guards expertly wielding their clubs, but had never bothered to practice these techniques afterwards.

"It is no use," said a young dwarf after trying hard with his club several times and succeeding only in bashing his own head each time.

"What do we do?" asked a female dwarf, holding her club clumsily.

"I think I have a good suggestion," said Fuam. "Let us capture one of the Mungongoh guards and compel him to train us in how to use these things. They have thorough expertise in the art."

"That is a risky thing to do," said a young dwarf. "How do we capture one of those tough guys and bring him down here?"

"Yes," said another dwarf, "who will be bold enough to do the capturing?"

"You are always easily defeated because you don't want to learn," said Fuam. "Listen to the cowardly way you talk. Those Mungongoh clowns are no way stronger than us. They are simply more organized."

"So what do we do?" asked Kanjam.

"We select about twenty strong dwarfs to do the capture together." said Fuam.

"Is that going to work?" asked another dwarf, dubiously.

"Sure," said Kanjam, now seeing Fuam's point. "We identify and isolate a guard and jump on him at once and suddenly. Then we tie him up with strong ropes and drag him down here. To them up there, our underground dwellings are like very complicated labyrinths. He will find it impossible to escape, and we will dispose of him whenever we consider that we no longer have use for him."

The other dwarfs were awed. None of them could have ever come up with an idea like that. They were very lucky to have fellow dwarfs operating deep inside enemy territory as palace servants.

"We should be very careful there," said another dwarf, who had once served in the palace. "He may come here, discover our secrets, and escape to reveal everything to the Ikwi. We don't want them to be alerted as surprise is one of the best weapons. Our captive must have no possibility of escaping."

Twenty of the strongest dwarfs were selected and placed under Fuam's control for the execution of this task. The Ikwi normally operated during daylight and slept at night. Palace guards, however, worked day and night. There were night shifts since the palace was supposed to be constantly guarded, especially now that the earthlings were allowed in Mungongoh on diplomatic missions. However, there was no strong enemy to guard the palace against. It was commonly known in Mungongoh that there were dwarf insurgents burning to strike at the least opportunity, but the dwarfs were considered disorganized and cowardly, thus minimizing any possible threat from them. Guarding the palace was seen as a formality. There were only two guards patrolling outside the palace walls and gate, while the others were concentrated inside. The two guards had booths on each side of the palace gates and, once every two hours, would leave these booths to walk around the wall until they met on the other side. Once they had ensured that there was no treat, they walked back to their booths. It was rather surprising that a palace with the capability of sophisticated means should employ such crude methods.

Awobua's lust for the Earth had made him overlook the possibility of peeping into the dwarfs dungeons, so no effort had been made in that direction. The dwarfs came out from their underground abode through a concealed hole not far from the palace and crept towards the palace gates. Each dwarf was carrying a length of stout rope made from dwarf hair. Dwarfs shaved their hair only when they needed to make ropes since their hair constituted the material for their ropes. Close to the palace gate, the dwarfs lay down for cover and watched the guards as they sat, each in his own booth.

"We shall take the one to the left," Fuam said.

At last the guards came out of their booths for their regular beats, wielding their clubs and moving away from each other. It never occurred to them that they were being watched or that there could be any change to the boring routine. Half way through his beat, however, the guard on the left side was surprised when twenty dwarfs pounced on him. As he struggled to raise the hand that carried the club, he received a serious blow from a huge stone that Fuam had carried along; other hands forcefully wrenched the club from his grasp. Then he felt stout ropes fastening his hands together and to his body. The blow had been quite vicious, and he was barely conscious.

Then the palace guard felt himself being lifted and carried along. He attempted to scream but discovered that stout ropes had also attached a dirty rag to his mouth, completely muffling any sound from there.

The dwarfs carried the palace guard to their concealed entrance into their underground network and lugged him along until they came to their underground training grounds. Other dwarfs were waiting at their appointed training ground. When the dwarfs brought the palace guard to this destination, they removed the gag from the palace guard's mouth and untied some of the ropes to permit him to sit up.

"What do you want?" he asked angrily.

It was the first time that such a thing had happened. Since he had been serving in the palace and even since he was born and grown up, he had always known that wild dwarfs were cowardly pilferers not kidnappers.

"What do you want from me you bunch of rascals?" the palace guard roared.

"You better watch your tongue," said Fuam. 'You are talking to your masters and should show some respect."

"Show some respect to who?' shouted the palace guard. "You must have gone crazy. Do you realize I am a Mungongoh citizen and a palace guard?"

"That is why you are here," said Fuam calmly. "Now stop bellowing like that bad boy Awobua and listen."

"Listen to who?" asked the palace guard, still surprised that the dwarfs would dare to kidnap him and take him to some unknown place. "Now let me advise you. Take me back to the palace before they miss me or you will be in serious trouble."

"Who will miss you?" asked Kanjam.

He and Tubuo had been afraid to show themselves and run the risk of being recognized by the palace guard. Now they were sure that their captive would not have any means to escape and go back to the palace.

"You guards are not of much importance," Kanjam said.

"Kanjam, it is you?" the palace guard asked him in surprise.

"Yes, it is me," replied Kanjam, "and you are our captive. If you try to escape, you will simply get lost inside our underground network."

"Why have you fellows brought me here?" the palace guard asked, still astonished.

"We want you to train us in the art of fighting with a club," said Fuam.

"Train you?" asked the palace guard. "But why? Who do you want to fight?"

"There," said Fuam. "That is a very stupid question. Who else but you Ikwi, who have usurped our planet, Jvatein, and have now given it some absurd name?"

"Mungongoh is not an absurd name," retorted the guard, "and I still don't know what you are talking about."

"You don't have to," said Fuam. "All you have to do is simply teach us how to use a club in combat."

"I'd rather use the club to bash in those massive skulls of yours," said the palace guard. "You seem to take me for some kind of traitor."

"What do we do with this fellow?" Fuam asked. "He is trying to prove he's tough."

"We could take out his eyes," Tubuo said, "and then practice the technique of clubbing enemies on him."

"That is a good idea," said Kanjam. "We could also use huge stones on his head. Bashing his head with stones will make him think positively."

"What hideous thing are you cooking up?" asked the frightened guard.

"Nothing serious." said Kanjam. "We are simply saying that you shall teach us how to fight. You are warned of dire consequences, however, if you attempt to hurt any of us."

The palace guard had no choice. It was not an easy task, but he had to be patient.

The dwarf leaders were the first to be trained. Then the palace guard continued to train an elite force under Fuam while each dwarf leader went back to train the dwarfs under his leadership. There were no soldiers and no difference between male and female. All were trained, apart from pregnant female dwarfs or breastfeeding dwarfs. Children, of course, were left out.

"That earthling really gave us a good idea," Fuam said to Kanjam. 'I am now certain that we will beat these Ikwi blokes after all."

"I have only one worry," said Kanjam.

"And what is that worry?" asked Fuam.

"The earthlings," said Kanjam. "Americans could be good allies, but they can abandon you when you least expect it."

"What are you trying to say?" asked Fuam.

'If the Mungongoh king discovers that the Americans are coming in to help us overthrow them, they may offer a better deal to the Americans and turn them on their side."

"That would be catastrophic," said Tubuo. "That would simply mean the end of the dwarfs. What a massacre would take place."

"Mungongoh cannot do without us though," said Kanjam. "They are counting on us for labour. Even the earthlings are aware of that."

"Let us consider a fall back strategy," said Tubuo. "If we are overwhelmed, what do we do?"

"We simply do what we have always done," said Fuam, "we slip underground."

"Ah, yes," said Kanjam. 'My father told me that by pilfering from Mongongoh citizens each time and dashing underground for cover, the Mungongli have been practicing escape tactics without realizing it. In their last battle with the Ikwi, before we were born, very few Mungongli were killed because most succeeded in escaping on time."

"Now,' said Fuam, "let us prepare for war."

The Mungongoh people were advanced in science; but, after the big bang in Mars, they had completely abandoned anything to do with warfare. Landing in Mungongoh, they had been compelled to fight against the dwarfs, but the dwarfs fought with their bare hands or used very crude objects like stones. It was not considered necessary to produce weapons. There was no hunting on Mungongoh either, so the need for spears, bows and arrows, or fire arms had never arisen. Other aspects of life were developed and high-tech in ways not yet imagined on Earth. But nothing destructive, such as bombs, guns, or ammunition, was ever considered. The only attempt to make anything destructive was under Awobua, and this was in his attempts to destroy the Earth. The laboratory of these items had been completely isolated, and was finally destroyed when Fulumfuchong came to power.

18

The members of the AIDM were all gathered in the main reception room in the palace watching a giant screen in expectance of the Americans.

"After today's meeting with the Americans," the king said, "the next meeting will be out there in America. Nyamfuka will attend this meeting with two others. We don't need a wonderfully big delegation. We are not like the earthlings, especially those of the lesser countries who carry along very large delegations just to go and discuss some trifling issue."

"Apart from that," said the queen, "this time we shall show them real Munghogoh hospitality. We shall entertain them well, and provide rooms here in the palace for them to spend the night. The President of America has been in touch with us, and I have personally been in touch with his wife. That black couple sounds very reassuring."

"Speaking with those two," continued the king, "gives you the impression that there are many upright persons in America. I suppose the villains mostly come from the white folk."

"There are equally many good white folk," said Ngess. "America is a land of extremes. They register the most violent crimes on earth and have the biggest crooks. They are into bad habits like drugs, sex displays, and bad language full of curses and obscenities. Contrary to this, they become seriously scandalized if an official figure so much as ogles a female that is not his wife. When it comes to government policy, they can be tricky and unreliable when the interests of America are at stake, but quite understanding and supportive if you are their ally and respect certain accepted norms and democratic principles."

"The President and his wife may be honest and respectful, but some of those blokes in the delegations that came here from America seem to be real knaves," said Funkuin. "I did not particularly like that General Steak."

"Maybe because he is a soldier or because of his stout structure?" said Ndaba. "But the real bad egg amongst them is that fishy character called Hawk."

"I agree with you," said Dr. Kini. "The chap is shifty-eyed and quite untrustworthy. While they were here, I had the impression that he was staring at everything in a concentrated manner, as if he were noting down information for some future use.

"That dubious fellow looked very much like a spy," Ndaba said insistently.

"I noticed something else that may be important," Dr. Kini said.

"What was it?" asked Nyamfuka.

"Hawk went to the toilet on the two occasions he was here and always asked the same dwarf to see him to the toilet."

"Is there anything wrong with that?" Nange asked

"I may be overreacting," said Kini, "but each time, the dwarf stayed slightly longer than usual before coming back to the hall."

"That does not say much," said Nyamfuka.

"Maybe," said Doctor Kini, "but the fact that on both occasions he called the same dwarf out of all the others is worth considering. Mind you, the fellow was not the closest dwarf to him the second time."

"That could mean something," said Ngess. "Which dwarf was it?" he asked one of the old senior dwarfs.

"It was Tubuo, sir," he replied.

Ngess had not been long in the palace, and his present high position did not warrant him to know dwarfs by name.

"And where is he?" asked Nyamfuka, looking at the dwarfs seating humbly in their corner, ready to serve.

"He did not report for duty today, sir," the dwarf replied.

"Did he give any reason?" Ngess asked.

Dwarfs never reported sick because they never fell ill. There was no way the dwarf could lie or protect him, but he tried.

"He had a serious fight with another dwarf, sir, and it was so bad that both of them could not report for duty."

"Who should this other dwarf be?" Ngess asked.

"Kanjam, sir. They tore each other up badly.

"Palace dwarfs fighting?" Kini asked. "That has never happened. I am aware of the fact that part of a dwarf's life is to engage in brawls after over-imbibing that blasted concoction they call ntop, but palace dwarfs have never stooped so low."

"I sensed something is wrong," Ngess said. "Some months ago, shortly after the last visit of the earthlings, one of our palace guards simply disappeared, and we have had no trace of him. Although it is an unusual happening, there was no real panic so there has not been much of a follow up."

Just then the large monitor relaying from the earth port blinked. This time the Americans were coming with their own space craft, which they had taken pains to perfect. The department of hate science had been scrapped and Earth-watching was no longer an important occupation and duty for the members of the AIDM. Neither was it any longer the favourite past-time of the king. Fulumfuchong preferred other pursuits, apart from governing and admiring his wife Yivissi.

Earth watching was no longer an obligatory task for the members of the defunct IRDI - now transformed into AIDM - so nobody had bothered to watch the progress made by the Americans in the construction of their space craft. What now appeared on the screen was a bit crude, but flying.

Inside the American space craft, Hawk emerged from his cubicle after making a secret phone call and moved to the pilots' station. As he opened the door and moved in, he removed a pistol from his pocket and pointed it at the pilots.

"What are you doing, sir?" the captain asked in surprise.

"Keep your mouth shut and do what I say," Hawk snapped, moving the direction of the pistol menacingly from one pilot to the other.

"Is this a highjack?" asked the co-pilot. "I thought these things only happened in airplanes on Earth."

"Stop asking stupid questions and obey orders," snarled Hawk.

The two pilots stood, confused, as Hawk started giving instructions.

"I am taking over this space craft," he said between clenched teeth. "You will do exactly as I instruct, and don't try to play smart with me. Any false move and I will blow those ugly skulls on your shoulders into splinters."

The pilots were now trembling in terror.

"Did all of you see that?" Ndaba was pointing at the large screen, which was now displaying the scene in the pilots' station.

"Something is certainly going wrong inside that spaceship," said Ngess.

"I am sure that the other passengers in the spacecraft are not aware of what is happening out there in that room," said Dr. Kini. "The Americans were right in always taking trained soldiers along with them. I only hope they will be capable of disarming that fellow before he causes any havoc."

"Get me a direct link to President Mboma of America," the king ordered.

The next minute, President Mboma was on the line.

"I am listening, brother," he said. "What is up?"

"This is quite urgent," the king said. "The diplomatic team you dispatched to us is under threat, and we are sure they are not yet aware of it. We use our high surveillance monitors on incoming craft and have identified the man Hawk as an enemy. Right now, he is holding the pilots at gunpoint and giving instructions as to their next move. Please get into contact with the leader of the team and inform him, but caution him to be careful. We are watching closely."

"The private phone in Mr. Dawson's room rang, and he jumped up almost to attention. It was the President.

"Yes, Mr. President?" he answered with respect.

"Hawk is taking over you spaceship," the President said.

"He has the pilots covered and is giving them instructions. Wait for further instructions but be careful."

From the Mungongoh palace, Hawks instructions to the pilot were being closely followed by the members of the AIDM, who concentrated on the monitor.

Dr. Kini, who had diverted his attention to another monitor, suddenly shouted.

"I think all of you should watch this. There is something else."

"I can see it," said Ngess, also switching over to the other monitor. "Two other crafts are also coming in. What do the Americans mean by this?"

"From every indication," said Fulumfuchong, "another nation or group of criminals on Earth have succeeded in accessing the blueprints of our space vessel from the

Americans and is using it to no good end. Get me President Mboma again."

The President of America was back on the line.

"Are you aware of the fact that two other spaceships are coming in alongside your own?" Fulumfuchong asked.

The President was surprised.

"Where do you suspect these other crafts would have come from?" asked King Fulumfuchong. "Did you give out the blueprints of our spaceships to some other country?"

"I would never do that, and the blueprints were kept safely," replied President Mboma. "I can't understand how this could have happened. I cannot even say who that intruder is. Out here on Earth we have our differences, but we don't go to such extremes. I believe no country, not even the Russians - our arch rivals - would go to this level."

"Don't worry, Mr. President," said the King. "We shall handle the situation from here. Permit us to contact Mr. Dubson and his crew directly."

"Thank you, Your Highness," said the President. "You have my full permission to work with my team out there."

"Switch over to the American space craft," the King said.

The switch was done immediately, and Mr. Dubson came on.

"Mr. Dubson," the king said, "you are fully aware of the situation in your spaceship, I suppose?"

"That is right, sir," Dubson replied. "We are still working out what to do."

"Don't do anything for now and stay in your rooms," the king instructed. "There are two enemy spaceships right behind you. We are closely following Hawk's instructions to the pilots and his communication with the enemy spacecraft."

"We shall be anxiously waiting, sir," Mr. Dubson said.

Everybody in the Mungongoh palace was attentive and quiet as they followed everything that Hawk said. Hawk was oblivious to the fact that his every word was entering the wrong ears. The dwarfs were even more attentive, but their expressions were as bland as usual.

After listening to Hawk, the king rapidly developed his own strategy. There was no time to start discussing and debating. Taking the right initiative now was imperative.

"Nyamfuka," the king said. "Go out with Dr. Kini and Ndaba and rally all the palace guards. Dr. Kini, take some of them to the earth port. The rest should assemble in front of the palace and wait for further orders from me."

The king turned to Ngess.

"Take over communication with Dubson. As you all heard, Hawk is aware of the procedure that when the plane lands, the passengers are allowed thirty minutes for their systems to adapt before they are asked to leave the spacecraft. During this period, everybody is expected to remain lying on a bunk. Hawk intends to take advantage of this, jump out of the craft as soon as it lands, and lock in all of the other passengers. As soon as their craft lands, the American soldiers should dash out and overpower this damned Hawk. A few of them may die in the process, but there is no other alternative."

He turned now to Funkuin.

"Now," he said, "the two of us shall go out and concentrate on the general coordination of the whole thing."

"What do we do?" asked Funkuin.

"The American soldiers are capable of fighting the intruders from the Earth. Our palace guards are on standby to intervene whenever possible. Now let us go out."

Outside, the king and members of the AIDM were met by loud whinnying sounds as dwarfs poured out of concealed

133

outlets from their underground abodes. They were all wielding crude clay clubs. While some were rushing into Mungongoh, a large group was moving towards the palace. Fuam, Kanjam, and Tubuo were leading this group.

"From every indication, we need all our palace guards here," the king said, shouting to Nyamfuka to act. Led by Nyamfuka and Ndaba, the palace guards assembled in front of the palace and rushed towards the dwarfs.

"Let us get two cars and move towards the earth port," the king told Funkuin.

At the earth port, heavy fighting had ensued with fire arms. Hawk had been overcome by Dubson and the American marines that were on the spaceship.

Led by instructions from Hawk, the enemy spacecraft had landed alongside the American one, and the mercenaries had jumped out and rushed towards the American craft, expecting to find it locked. They had come with explosives with which they planned to blow up the craft, along with its human cargo. Great was their surprise when they rushed into American marines who were firing freely. Before the mercenaries could regain their stance, many of them had been struck down. Others who were carrying explosives exploded along with the volatile stuff as flying bullets set them off. Fighting raged on for a while, but the few remaining mercenaries finally surrendered. The element of surprise had worked greatly to the advantage of the Americans. Again, the mercenaries had anticipated an easy battle with the Americans and the Mungongoh citizens, since they expected to have the dwarfs on their side. They were thus dressed only in military fatigues and berets and were quite exposed to the flying bullets of the Americans. The marines for their part were all well-protected with helmets and bullet-proof jackets. The few who received lethal bullets were the unfortunate ones who happened to have received direct hits on the head and neck.

"It was a complex plot," the king told Dubson, who had come to meet him. "The dwarfs are also trying to take over the town, and this time they have clubs and seem to be better organized. We need the assistance of your marines. Tell them that they don't need to shoot. They should simply use the butt of their guns to club the dwarfs into submission."

Around the palace the dwarfs were almost jubilant. The palace guards were fighting hard but were far outnumbered by the dwarfs. Elsewhere Mungongoh citizens were overwhelmed by club wielding dwarfs and ran for cover.

Suddenly, the American marines arrived after quickly subduing the mercenaries at the earth port. They were well-trained and had better clubbing instruments. Besides, they could kick, dish out karate chops, duck or feint, and block blows from the crude clubs of the dwarfs without much effort.

Fuam had just bitten off the ear of a Mungongoh palace guard, who had reacted by dropping his club and placing his freed hands on the bleeding spot where his ear had been. As he was howling in pain and unprotected, Fuam landed a savage blow on his head with her club and continued pounding as the palace guard crumbled to the ground. She looked up in victory and found a burly American standing in front of her. Fuam was quick to react. She jumped up and landed a powerful blow on the head of the American, but the blow simply glanced off his helmet as he stood smiling. The American could not react immediately. He was surprised that such a gnarled old female could fight with such violence and vigour. Fuam took advantage of this and landed another powerful blow with her club, which the American blocked with the butt of the fire arm that he was carrying. This is when the disadvantages of weapons moulded with clay and baked became evident. As the club landed against the solid butt of the gun, it shattered into so many pieces. Fuam was now left unarmed. She turned and attempted to dash for safety, but was tripped by Nyamfuka who had been keenly following her activities. He was sure this was the dreaded dwarf leader they called Fuam. His attempt to pick her up met with such a violent and dangerous resistance that the American marine had to step in and administer a few jabs with the butt of his gun, smashing Fuam's skull into a messy mush.

Fighting quickly swayed in favour of Mungongoh. Tubuo, who did not quite understand what was happening, found himself regretting bitterly that he had ever dared to trust an earthling. After Fuam's demise, Kanjam and Tubuo, who had also been fighting right in front were finally clubbed to death, by American marines. The dwarfs suddenly burst into a disorderly rush to escape for dear life and many dwarfs sustained serious injury in the process.